A FRIGH[illegible]

"And bring back a tray of tea and small cakes, Earline." I surprised myself giving orders. "Don't lollygag as you usually do or I'll slap you good. You hear?"

Earline dragged her feet and swished out of the room. "Yes, miss, I'm a-goin'."

"And don't you dare stop and talk to anyone, either," I called after her. "Or I'll tell Dr. McGill and he'll punish you good."

I don't even need lessons, I thought. *I'm good at this.* Then I was frightened. It was easy, too easy. Is this how simple it was for people in the South? How ordinary? And tempting to do every day?

Aunt Susan Elizabeth used to say there was something in all of us that delighted in bullying those lower in the social order of things. And that was what made slavery so easy for the white folks to practice.

My father said fear is what made it easy to practice. That down in the Deep South there were places where the blacks outnumbered the whites. And the whites had to keep them under control.

Both reasons frightened me. Because whatever my reason was, I was good at it.

Other Novels by Ann Rinaldi

Leigh Ann's Civil War

My Vicksburg

The Letter Writer

Juliet's Moon

Come Juneteenth

An Unlikely Friendship
A Novel of Mary Todd Lincoln and Elizabeth Keckley

Brooklyn Rose

Or Give Me Death
A Novel of Patrick Henry's Family

The Staircase

The Coffin Quilt
The Feud between the Hatfields and the McCoys

Cast Two Shadows
The American Revolution in the South

An Acquaintance with Darkness

Hang a Thousand Trees with Ribbons
The Story of Phillis Wheatley

Keep Smiling Through

The Secret of Sarah Revere

Finishing Becca
A Story about Peggy Shippen and Benedict Arnold

The Fifth of March
A Story of the Boston Massacre

A Break with Charity
A Story about the Salem Witch Trials

A Ride into Morning
The Story of Tempe Wick

The Ever-After Bird

Ann Rinaldi

HOUGHTON MIFFLIN HARCOURT
Boston New York

www.hmhco.com

The Library of Congress has cataloged the hardcover edition as follows:

Rinaldi, Ann.

The Ever-After Bird/Ann Rinaldi.

p. cm.

Summary: In 1851, thirteen-year-old Cecelia has her eyes opened to the horrors of slavery when she accompanies her ornithologist uncle on an expedition in search of the rare scarlet ibis, and watches as he shows slaves the way to the Underground Railroad.

[I. Uncles—Fiction. 2. Scarlet ibis—Fiction. 3. Birds—Fiction. 4. Slavery—Fiction. 5. Underground Railroad—Fiction. 6. Georgia—History—1775–1865—Fiction.] I. Title.

PZ7.R459Ev 2007

[Fic]—dc22 2006101592

HC ISBN-13: 978-0-15-202620-2

PA ISBN-13: 978-0-547-25854-6

Text set in Adobe Garamond

Printed in the United States of America

DOH 10 9 8 7 6 5 4 3

4500634119

To our dear friends
Marcia and Dave

The Ever-After Bird

Chapter One

I TRY NOT to think of that morning in May of this year of 1851. It is muddled in my brain anyway, maybe because I choose to leave it muddled. I did not see it all, I tell myself. I was upstairs in my room in our rambling white farmhouse, sent upstairs by Papa because I sassed Aunt Susan Elizabeth. She was Papa's aunt, getting on in years and in grouchiness.

She drove me to distraction and I would have given anything to be away from her, from that house, yes, even from Papa, who had few words of cheerfulness for me since the day I was born and fewer yet since he'd become involved with his abolitionist doings, which seemed like forever now.

He went about those doings with an obsession.

There was always a quilt on the front wooden fence to show we were a safe house for runaways. I know because I put them there for Aunt Susan Elizabeth.

We had five of those quilts, and the ones on the fence were constantly changed.

The quilts said things.

Each one had a different message. What, I don't know because I could never quite learn the differences. It had to do with the square knots left visible on the front, which Aunt Susan Elizabeth said was usually the sign of shoddy workmanship.

But not with these quilts. These square knots were left on the front on purpose.

The quilts each had a set number of square knots. She must have explained to me a dozen times the many things those knots meant. But I never got it. Which made her call me "dense."

I hated those quilts because I was always having to work on one. That morning I was working on a wagon wheel pattern, which Aunt Susan Elizabeth said signaled the slaves to pack everything that would go into a wagon or that could be used in transit.

"Why can't they just be told?" I asked her. It wasn't so much the words I said as how I said them.

That's when Papa sent me to my room.

"No soul," he said to me, "you've got no soul. For

this your mother gave her life when you were born. No soul."

He'd been saying a lot of things like that to me lately, because I refused to get involved with his abolitionist doings. I couldn't understand him risking his life for all those negroes who came to our door in the middle of the night looking like something the cat dragged in.

Two nights before he'd taken in two runaways from the Harris plantation in Buckstown, Maryland, a state part slave and part free.

They'd had enough of old Mr. Josiah Harris's cruelty.

We live in the small town of Christiana, Pennsylvania, on the Maryland border. My name is Cecelia McGill. Papa's name is John. Runaway negroes know we're a station on the Underground Railroad.

It was a bright morning, about ten o'clock. I was sitting on my bed, wondering how long I'd have to stay there, when I heard horses ride up. I went to look out the window.

It was Mr. Harris and he had his two mangy sons with him. I pushed the window open so I could hear. Harris was waving around a paper, which apparently was some kind of a writ. "Signed under the new Fugitive Slave Act of 1850, McGill," I heard him yell. "Gives me the right to cross over into another state and pursue and take back the runaways."

My father said something; I didn't hear what. The Harrises got off their horses and headed for the house. I heard my father tell them to wait outside, then he must have come in and gone to the secret hiding place under the parlor and brought the slaves up, because he's nothing if not a law-abiding man, my father. He brought them outside.

Then more men rode up. I recognized the Wallers, Quakers from the area. More trouble. I don't know why people have to force their beliefs on everybody else, why they just can't practice them and leave others alone.

Right off the Quakers started with the thees and thous, challenging the legality of the whole thing. An argument started. It got loud. Soon there was pushing and shoving. One of the Harrises fired his gun in the air. The horses jumped and got antsy. Then more guns went off.

It all happened very fast. And of a sudden I saw my papa fall on the ground and the Harrises mount their horses and gallop away and the Quakers mount their horses, and for all their thees and thous pay no attention to my father but take the slaves on the horses behind them and whisk them off. Likely in the direction of the next safe house and on to Canada.

And I, who have no soul, went downstairs to see if my father was alive or dead.

Chapter Two

I DON'T RECALL the next couple of days, except in a whirl of mixed-up activity. The Wallers sent over a container of chicken soup. Others sent roasted potatoes, preserves from their gardens all done up in their favorite recipes, cakes and pies, even syllabubs. Felicity York came from across the Two Horse Creek. She had her "man" drive her right to the front door, then sent him home again.

"I've come to help," she announced to Aunt Susan Elizabeth. I could see Aunt wasn't overly fond of the idea, but she acquiesced as if Felicity were some kind of long-lost relative. And had rights. There was something about Felicity York that was different, that commanded attention, if not always the good kind. She was like a woman with a "past," only nobody spoke about what it was.

Besides, Aunt needed help. Somebody had to sort out all the food and oversee our maids, Constance and Ginny. Aunt seemed torn, beset by Felicity's presence and yet relieved. In between all this she was making me a dress for the funeral. I recollect, vaguely, trying it on.

Short sleeves, black, full skirt. I didn't care if I went in pants with suspenders. I still didn't believe Papa was dead. I expected him to come in from the barn any minute and tell me I had no soul. I was finding out that you don't have to love somebody to miss them.

Then before you know it, Aunt was having Ginny and Constance set the dining room table as it used to be set of a Sunday, "when your mama was alive," she said. With her good china and silver and crystal that hadn't been used since I came along.

You could almost see the line drawn in the dust on the plates.

Before I came along and after.

"After your mama passed, your pa shut down," Felicity told me when we were alone in the kitchen. "You should have known him before."

Her man came around again with two cooked turkeys.

Then came Uncle Alex and Aunt Elise. She came with a chair with wheels because of "the accident." Another thing people spoke of in whispers. Something about her getting thrown out of the carriage Uncle Alex had been driving when it swerved because he'd been staring at a bird.

She got crippled. And their son had been killed.

I hadn't seen them in years. He was Papa's much-younger brother, and all I'd been told by Papa was that they "didn't much get on."

I had distant memories here. Of a young boy holding my hand, teaching me to walk, playing at marbles with me. And then, I was told, when I was three, he went away to school.

Too many things were shrouded in secrecy in my family. And I was now left with nothing but questions I dared not ask.

Uncle Alex was tall and well built. He lifted Aunt Elise right out of that carriage and put her in her chair with wheels and brought her in the house.

"Hello, everybody," he said. Too cheerful for somebody who had made his wife a cripple and killed his son.

Too cheerful for this family. He would never fit here, I decided.

His hair was longish and curly in front. He had to push it aside. His eyes were sad and didn't go with the rest of him. I'd heard that now he was a doctor and an expert on birds.

And an abolitionist. Like Papa.

There was nodding and hellos and kisses and shaking of hands, for more people had come. I noticed that Felicity did not come out of the dining room but stayed away. I hung back.

"CeCe?" Uncle Alex came away from the back of Aunt Elise's chair. "Is that you? I haven't seen you in years." He put an arm around me and kissed me. "How you've grown." He led me over to Aunt Elise. She was blond and wore her hair long and in a single braid down her back. She was beautiful. Her eyes smiled. Somebody had told me she worked all the time on those darned quilts that said things.

"Want to talk to you later, after the funeral," Uncle Alex whispered in my ear.

At the small Presbyterian Church, Felicity was in tears. I was too numb for tears. I couldn't have told anyone how I got into the black silk with the small white collar that Aunt Susan Elizabeth had sewn up for me over the last two days.

Afterward, at the church cemetery, when they put my father in the ground next to my mama and I couldn't cry, I felt embarrassed. I caught Uncle Alex looking at me as he twirled his hat around in his hands.

He wasn't looking so sad, either. What was it they'd told me? My father had brought him up since he was twelve when their parents were drowned on a trip to England when the boat sank. And now they didn't get on so well.

What had happened?

After we ate, on tables set outside under the trees because it was a lovely July day, Aunt Susan Elizabeth told me it would behoove me to speak with Uncle Alex after everyone had gone home.

The guests left finally when the sun got low and the mosquitoes came out. Uncle Alex picked Aunt Elise right up in his arms and she said good night. I followed them in as he carried her upstairs to bed and fixed the mosquito netting around her.

Back downstairs Uncle Alex lit lamps that sent a pleasant glow. Aunt made more coffee and left me at the dining room table, which had been cleared.

Uncle Alex came over and sat down. "We should talk," he said.

I nodded, getting more scared by the minute.

"You see, CeCe, it's like this. Your father left a simple will. He left this whole place to you, but since you are underage, he left it in my care, and we are always to make it a home for Aunt Susan Elizabeth as long as she lives."

"Yes, sir," I said.

"And he's left you to my care, too."

"Am I like the farm?" I asked. "Left to your care?"

He didn't get angry, though perhaps he should have. "You're more valuable than the farm to your aunt Elise and me. We'd very much like for you to come and live with us."

I felt ashamed. His eyes continued to look sad. "Well now," and he lowered his voice, "I hear you and your aunt don't always get on."

I had the decency to blush. "She's your aunt, too."

"Ah, a saucy little piece, is it? What is it then that attracts you so here, aside from the fact that it's your home?"

"My dog, Skipper," I said. "And my cat, Patches, and my horse, Pelican."

"Well, you could certainly bring them with you if you came with us to Ohio."

I looked down, ashamed. "I couldn't cry at Papa's funeral," I said.

He nodded. "Sometimes people cry later."

I shook my head no. "He said I had no soul. He hated me. He blamed me for Mama's death."

He bit his lower lip. "We can talk about that sometime."

I was afraid to say more. "The reason I want to live here is so I can go to the Artsdale Female Seminary in another year when I'm old enough."

"And for another year continue to argue with Aunt

Susan Elizabeth? She's getting on in years. I'm responsible for both of you. I can't let you make her last years hell."

"I'll be good."

"No you won't. I know because I never was at your age. And I see a lot of me in you. Anyway, at that Artsdale Female Seminary all you'll learn is how to pour tea and attract boys. I'd rather see you go to Oberlin College. I'm a trustee there. You'd get a real education. Listen, I've got a proposition to make to you."

He was going on a trip, he said. Next month. He was going on one of his bird expeditions. South. To Georgia.

"I'm going to find and sketch birds that have never been sketched before. It's what I do besides doctoring. I stay at Southern plantations. They open their homes to me and my assistant, and we go out into the fields and the woods and find birds and I paint them. I'm called an ornithologist."

"I thought you were a doctor."

He smiled. "I'm both. Your father made me study to be a doctor. I always wanted to paint birds. He said I could do that in my spare time. So I do. Now I'm proposing you come on this trip with me. Help me out. See how they live down South. I hear you want nothing to do with being an abolitionist."

"My father was obsessed with it. And the more he got involved the surlier he became."

"Yes, well, you don't think the negroes should be free?"

"I think people should do as they want and let others do as they want."

"Ah, you're a freethinker. You'd fit in well at Oberlin. Well, what do you say? You want to come with me?"

"You can't change my mind. About being an abolitionist."

"I can help you make up your mind. That will be the purpose of the trip. And if, when we get back, you decide you don't want to live with me, you can continue to live here with Aunt Susan Elizabeth and go to Artsdale. I'll let the decision be yours."

"Really?"

"Yes. You seem mature enough to make that decision. How old are you, anyway?"

"Fourteen."

"You're not. I was fifteen when you were born and I'm twenty-eight. You're thirteen. Don't lie. People find out."

"Do you remember when I was born?"

"Yes."

"Was I christened?"

"Yes."

"Then I do have a soul."

His whole face went as sad as his eyes then. "Oh,

child," he said. "What did he do to you?" And he sighed. "The same thing, I see, that he tried to do to me."

We talked a bit more. He said no more about my father, but I sensed he knew secrets that nobody else knew. He let me talk and have my say, too.

"Who is your assistant?" I asked finally.

"You'll like her. She's a student at Oberlin, looking to get some extra credit. You two can learn some things from each other."

He smiled. He did have a lovely smile. Sort of crooked and pleading.

Still, I stalled, like a donkey refusing to come out of the gate. It was nice being asked, instead of gruffly ordered.

"One more thing I should mention," he said casually. "There's a particular bird I'm searching for on this trip. It's been said it's extinct, but I don't believe so. It's called the scarlet ibis by the experts. Or *Eudocimus ruber* in Latin. The slaves call it the Ever-After Bird."

I liked that. "Why?"

"Because they say when they sight it, they will be free ever after."

I sat still, nodding my head. "Do you think you'll find it?"

"Yes."

I told him, yes, sir, I'll go with you. But I had to ask Aunt's permission first.

"Only permission you need is mine from here on in," he reminded me.

It seemed strange, but not entirely unpleasant. I could work around him, I decided. Anybody with those sad eyes and that smile could be worked around. After all, I'd lived with Papa, hadn't I?

Chapter Three

I AM A great believer in listening at closed doors. I learned most of what I know about my family that way since nobody in my house was ever honest with me.

They always talked in riddles, giving out just enough information to tantalize me. And for all his honesty and crooked smile and for all her beauty and patience, Uncle Alex and Aunt Elise were turning out the same way.

I just happened to be in my nightgown outside Papa's door that night. They were using his bedroom. If caught I could always lie and say I was going downstairs for some milk.

I was good at lying. It had saved me from many a whipping from Papa, who kept his riding crop hanging behind the kitchen door.

Aunt Elise and Uncle Alex were talking in loud, whispered tones.

"You didn't tell her the whole of it, Alex?" from Aunt Elise.

"No. Not yet."

"But you said you wanted her to trust you."

"There's time to tell her. I'll pick the right time on the trip. There are so many things I have to tell her. She's confused about a lot. I'll parcel it out when I sense she's ready. She's had too much to take in just now. I've yet to see her smile."

"Her father just died, Alex."

"She didn't love him."

"How can you say that?"

"He didn't love her. He beat her. I saw the same riding crop behind the kitchen door that he used on me. I've got to bring her around. She trusts no one. I've got to gain her trust first. And I will. She's made of good parts."

I felt a warmth toward Uncle Alex then. No one had ever tried to understand me.

"Oh, I wish I could go with you, darling," Aunt Elise said.

"I know. I hate leaving you." His words were muffled then. I moved away from the door and started back to my room. I do have some decency in me, after all.

WE STAYED for two more days. There were things Uncle Alex had to do. After all, the farm was in his name now, until I came of age. He inspected it with Mr. Wiggins, the foreman, who lived with his wife and small son in a cottage nearby.

He brought me along with him, too. So I could learn, he said.

He was surprised at what I knew: what time the cows got milked, how the milk got put out front for pickup. Where it went. How many hogs we had and when they went to market. What yield the cornfields would bring, and so forth.

He was impressed, and Mr. Wiggins told him, thinking he was out of earshot of me, "She's a smart little girl. The mister never gave her full credit. Glad you're takin' over, sir. Me and the missus will report to Miz Susan Elizabeth every day."

THE MORNING of our departure, at breakfast, Uncle Alex excused himself and signaled that I was to come along with him. "Where are your scissors, Aunt?" he asked.

I thought it had something to do with quilts.

"Which ones do I cut?" he asked.

"Just leave the ones in front of the house," she requested.

"Come on, CeCe."

I followed him outside, around the back to the kitchen garden, where the last of Aunt Susan Elizabeth's lilacs were still in full bloom. He cut a nice bouquet and handed it to me. "Put it in the carriage," he directed.

I did so.

"Now say good-bye to your dog and cat. I'll get Aunt Elise."

We'd agreed that we'd come back for my dog and cat after the trip, if I decided to stay with him. I shed some tears, saying good-bye. He gave me time for those tears and said not a word.

We took my horse, Pelican. Uncle Alex had examined him, running his practiced hands all over his back and down his legs, and said he'd do fine on the trip. Then he told me to ride in the carriage with Aunt Elise. Pelican would be tethered in back. I wanted to ride Pelican, alongside the carriage, but I figured I'd best obey Uncle Alex. He looked solemn as he oversaw our leave-taking, as if he would brook no arguments.

"Say good-bye to Aunt Susan Elizabeth," he directed, "and tell her you're sorry for all the hell-raising you did."

"I never . . ."

He was checking the harnesses of the two horses that

pulled the carriage. Quickly he turned and gave me a look that said more than Papa's riding crop ever had.

"Yes, sir," I said.

Aunt Susan Elizabeth was putting a basket of food into our carriage. I hugged her. "I'm sorry for all the times I misbehaved," I said.

She shook her gray head and tucked my unruly hair behind my ears. "It's difficult enough growing up, never mind doing it without a mother," she told me.

Uncle Alex came up behind us. He waited, turned away.

"Well, I am sorry. I know I was bad sometimes. Papa always said I was a thorn in his side."

She hugged me again. "I never had my own children, so I don't know how to be a mother."

I started to cry.

"Come now. It isn't as if we won't be seeing each other again. I'm only sixty-five. Why, I'll wager you'll come back all grown up. Associating with your uncle Alex here will do that for you. Just remember everything I tried to teach you, and obey him."

"Yes, ma'am."

Uncle Alex hugged her then. "I'll take good care of her, don't worry. You take care of yourself. Get in the carriage, CeCe."

They talked a while longer. Serious-like. Then he came and got up on the driver's seat and we started down the road.

There was a quilt on the wooden fence. The nine patch design. I'd worked on it. There were nine gardening patches on it. I'd done three. Nine referred to the number of safe houses, including ours, to which the runaways would be taken. I ached inside, looking at that quilt. The farm looked so pretty as we drove away.

We made one stop, at the church we attended. Why was I surprised? We stopped at the burying ground and Uncle Alex got out and bade me bring the bouquet of lilacs. I knew then what he was up to. And I didn't move.

"Come on, CeCe, we've a long ride ahead of us."

"Do I have to?"

"Yes," he said solemnly, "you do."

"Why?"

"Don't ask me why when I tell you to do things, CeCe," he said kindly, but with firmness. "But in this instance I will tell you why. Because you'll feel a lot better inside yourself if you do. Now come along."

I went with him. He held my hand as we made our way through the grave sites to Papa's. The earth around his grave was still freshly dug up and there was no tombstone yet.

"Go put them down," he said.

I put the peonies on the center of the grave. Then he knelt and gestured that I should, too. "Say a prayer," he directed. "To yourself."

I did so, and slithering my eyes to the side I saw he was doing so, too. That touched me and made me feel better. If he could do it, I could do it, I decided. And while I was doing it, I said, *Thank you, God, for Uncle Alex. And please help me to be good to him.*

Chapter Four

UNCLE ALEX'S house was in Ripley, Ohio, on a three-hundred-foot-high bluff overlooking the Ohio River. It had lamps in every one of its windows, which could be seen far across the river in Kentucky by runaway slaves.

Uncle kept the lamps lit only when it was safe for them to seek him out. The slaves needed lights for when they would be crossing the river, and climbing the steep bluff on the stairs he'd built going up to his house.

The trip to his house took us two days. We stopped at a fashionable inn in Ohio where Uncle Alex knew the innkeeper, who, I think, was part of the Underground Railroad, too. Uncle Alex told me there were over two hundred underground homes in Ohio. After Aunt Elise and I went to bed, he stayed up late downstairs talking with the innkeeper.

Everybody, it seemed, liked Uncle Alex. Everybody in the inn seemed to know him, either through his interest in birds or his doctoring or his abolitionist doings.

We arrived at his home at sunset. The house, large and comforting, with a front porch spreading its arms out for visitors and a barn in back, beckoned to us. Someone was already lighting the last of the lamps in the front windows while the red and purple streaked sky in the west made a painter's backdrop for the house.

"Earline must know there're no slave hunters in the area tonight," Uncle Alex said. "Well, welcome to our home, CeCe."

The carriage drew up in front and a white male servant came out to take charge of the horses.

"Pelican needs to be fed," I said.

"Charlie knows what to do," Uncle told me.

A negro woman appeared on the porch. "Welcome home," she said.

Did he have slaves, then? I gaped. Who was this?

A heavyset white woman came to assist with Aunt Elise. Uncle Alex introduced me. "This is Nancy," he said. "You'd best make friends with her. And abide by her wishes or you don't eat around here. Nancy, this is my niece, CeCe McGill. She'll be with us for a few days before we leave on our trip."

"Little girl doesn't look as big as her name. Looks like

she needs a fattening up," Nancy said. "Supper's almost ready. Come on in and wash up."

The negro girl came over and Uncle Alex introduced me to her in the same way. "Earline, this is CeCe. I told you about her. Why don't you take her into the house and get her cleaned up for supper?"

"Yes, sir," Earline said.

You never know with people, I thought. They talk good talk about saving the negroes, but when it comes down to it, they have a black servant hidden away in some closet in their houses, someone to wait on them hand and foot.

I was disappointed in Uncle Alex. He ought to stand for what he preached.

Maybe, I thought, maybe she's a runaway, and he's sending her to Canada. But no, she'd be hidden in some secret passageway if she were.

Earline picked up one of my portmanteaus, and I waited for her to pick up the other. She didn't.

"Come on," Uncle Alex said. "We have no princesses around here. You take one, CeCe."

My face flushed and I picked up the other and followed Earline into the house.

My room was on the second floor in front, and from the open window I could smell the river. Earline extinguished the lamps, saying something about fire.

"Doctor is careful," she said.

"You call him Doctor?"

"What else would I call him?" She was unpacking the contents of my portmanteau, taking out my nightgowns and underclothes. In the other were my dresses and petticoats and shawls and bonnets. I set to working with her.

"Such pretty clothes," she said. "But you didn't answer. What do you think I should call your uncle?"

"Isn't he your master?" I asked quietly.

She stood ramrod straight. Everything about her went rigid. "You think I'm a slave? His slave?"

"Well, yes, I thought . . ."

She laughed, then bit her lower lip, and I thought she would cry. "You think him dishonest then. That he speaks out of both sides of his mouth. You do him a dishonor. He is a good man."

She was silent for a moment. Then she spoke again. "I am a student at Oberlin College."

"You're his assistant."

"Yes."

She was haughty, proud. She stood, tall and straight, her black hair cut short. Of course. How could you wash long hair on a trip? She had high cheekbones and a firm mouth. Her eyes were almost almondlike. I should apologize. But something about her, some pride I did not have and knew I never could have, kept me from doing it.

How dare she have such pride? Is this what happened to negroes when they were freed? Is this what my father was shot for?

She gestured to the washbasin on the nightstand. "There's warm water and soap. You'd best wash and comb your hair. That blue dress there is perfect for supper. Your uncle is very particular." She laughed. "He likes neatness. Wait until you see some of his drawings."

I RESENTED THAT she knew him better than I did. He was my uncle after all.

She stopped at the door. "He doesn't like tardiness. A word of advice. Don't make him angry. You won't like the results."

"Are you going to tell him?" My voice failed.

"That you thought me his slave? Oh, he'll appreciate that, yes, he will. Hurry down now." And she went out the door.

Now I was frightened. Here I was miles from home, and tired and hungry and scared. I had offended Uncle Alex's assistant, of whom he thought the world. He'd referred to her in fond tones at least a dozen times on the trip here. Trouble was, he'd said "my assistant" and not "Earline." How was I to know she was negro?

What was I to do now? I washed my face and hands and combed my hair and put on the blue dress, vexed to find she'd picked the one with the buttons down the back. I slipped it on and tried to button it. But couldn't. At home, Aunt Susan Elizabeth always had to help me. Looking through my portmanteau I saw why Earline had picked the dress. All the others were wrinkled.

What to do now? Likely they were waiting for me to come down to start dinner. How could I make such a disaster of things on my first night here?

Don't make him angry. You won't like the results.

I sat on the bed and gave in to my miseries and cried. I missed home, my own room, my pets, Aunt Susan Elizabeth, and even my father telling me I had no soul. There was a familiarity about it all that I yearned for. My life before was gone. And now here I was in the wilds of Ohio with an uncle I was afraid of and a negro girl who was haughty and a dress I couldn't button.

I didn't hear footsteps, but there was a soft knock on the door. Then before I could answer, he came in. Uncle Alex.

Why hadn't I noticed how tall he was before? How broad of shoulder, how his presence changed the room from one of hopelessness to one of life?

"Are you sick, CeCe? Have you been brought low by the trip?"

I wiped my face with my hand. "No, sir."

"Then why aren't you coming down to dinner?"

I balled my fists at my sides to keep from trembling. Surely he must know by now that I'd thought Earline a slave. *Don't make him angry. You won't like the results.*

"I can't button my dress in back. Aunt Susan Elizabeth always did it."

He crossed the room in what seemed like two strides. "In heaven's name, stand up." He towered over me.

"Are you going to beat me?"

He scowled. "Am I supposed to?"

"Papa would."

"At least tell me what for."

"Because I treated Earline like she was a slave. Because I thought you kept a negro slave."

He sighed and rubbed his forehead. "I only do beatings on Thursdays," he said. "Now for god's sake get up and turn around so I can button your dress. I'm about starved."

I did so. And he buttoned it, carefully. There were about twelve tiny buttons and he asked who in hell made such a dress and I told him Aunt made it and he said, well, don't bring it on the trip, I'll not do this again. And I thanked him. Then he turned me around and took out his handkerchief and wiped the tears from my face and smoothed back my hair and sat down in a nearby chair and, holding both my wrists, drew me over to him.

"Earline and I were both really delighted that you thought her a slave," he said. "You want to know why?"

I said yes.

"I can't bring a free negro along to those Georgian plantations. It just isn't done. They simply wouldn't tolerate it. Or me. They'd likely sell her off right in front of my nose to a slave dealer. So what do I do? We have to pretend she's a slave. My slave. She has to dress and play the part. And you and I have to treat her that way."

My eyes widened.

"I was going to tell you later on, on the trip. But this is the perfect time."

"So I did the right thing?"

"No, you did the wrong thing. And I'm disappointed in you. First because you assumed that just because she's a negro she's a slave. And second because you thought that I dishonored my way of life by keeping a slave in secret."

"I'm sorry, Uncle Alex."

"I think you should apologize to Earline."

I lowered my head. "I don't want to."

"And why is that?"

"She's . . . she thinks she's better than me. She acts superior. She lords it over me because she knows more about you than I do. And you're *my* uncle, not hers."

He smiled. "Ah, we have a female jealousy problem here. Well, I promise you'll get to know me on this trip. Maybe more than is to your liking. As for Earline, it's all a front. She puts herself forward because she's really afraid inside. Do you know that she's a runaway? That she suffered cruelty as a slave? That she was beaten? Ask her, why don't you. I think you two could become friends. I think you could learn a lot from her."

I said nothing. I'd been beaten. And I'd never been a slave. Did negroes think they had the corner on mistreatment?

"I want you to apologize to her," he said again. And this time the tone brooked no argument. "Don't let me hear that you didn't."

Don't make him angry. You won't like the results.

"Yes, sir," I said. And we went down to dinner.

Chapter Five

"I'M SORRY I treated you as if you were a slave." I stood there in the doorway of her room. It was the next morning. She was making her bed. She went right on making it and did not answer. What did I do now? I had never apologized to a negro before.

The only negroes I'd had to do with were the ones my father had taken in of a night to keep until morning. And then from a distance.

It came to me then that I'd never spoken to one of them.

"Earline?"

"I heard you."

"Is it all right? Can I go now?"

"Where are you going? I see you're dressed for riding."

"I'm taking Pelican out to exercise him."

She put her hands on her hips and sighed heavily. "No, you're not."

"What?"

"Your uncle said I could punish you. So I say no riding today. You're to stay inside and study."

I could not believe this. "Uncle Alex said that? I don't believe it."

"You want to ask him and find out?"

"Yes." I turned to go.

"Wait. He's not in a good mood. I wouldn't advise it."

I stopped and turned around and stared at her. What was she doing? And then it came to me. She didn't like me any more than I liked her. But being older, and being necessary to Uncle Alex, she had the upper hand. And she knew it.

But no riding? I had to listen to her?

"It isn't my idea. It's your uncle's. I'd say you'd best obey. Here." She handed me a pamphlet. I glanced at it. It was all about abolitionists and freed negroes in Philadelphia.

"You're to study it and by the end of the day tell him how many freed negroes there are in Philadelphia. How many own property and what the North Star has to do with the whole thing."

I threw it on the floor. "I won't. Apologizing to you

was bad enough. I'm not taking orders, too. I'm going riding."

Quickly she picked up the pamphlet. "You don't understand. This is a sort of test from your uncle. You're going to have to learn to take orders from me if you go on this trip. We all have to act in concert with one another, and if there's any dissension, things could go awry and everything could go wrong."

It all sounded right for a minute, but I still didn't trust her. Why didn't Uncle Alex warn me about all this? He was an honest, decent man. And by now I'd just about decided I would do anything he asked me to do to help him.

She handed the pamphlet to me and I took it. "More than all that, your uncle wants you to study in his studio," she told me. "It's the room at the end of the hall."

I went down the hall to a room with wide-paned windows and bare wooden floors and easels all around and sketches of birds. Beautiful sketches, some finished in watercolors to take one's breath away, some just done in pencil.

There was the *White Ibis*. And the *Little Blue Heron*. There were dozens of books and all his supplies. In the corner were his guns. On his desk were papers and lists and letters to people in England. In a corner on a shelf were half a dozen stuffed birds.

In another corner, in a standing gold-colored cage, was a small bird with a gray back and gray and black tail feathers. It had brown, sad eyes.

Somehow I felt that I shouldn't be here. The whole room was like a shrine to Uncle Alex's work. I felt as if I were intruding, but I also felt fascinated, as if I was privy to a part of him now that I wasn't allowed to see before. Maybe that's what he'd wanted.

I made myself sit down in the chair and read the pamphlet. It was all about Philadelphia. And how many freed negroes lived there. And how many owned property. It had stories of the escapes of slaves on the Underground Railroad. And then finally I found the business about the North Star.

I don't know how many hours went by, but I did another tour of the room, and I was just about to touch some watercolor brushes when a voice barked behind me.

"What are you doing in here?"

I turned to see Uncle Alex.

"Well?"

"I've been studying, like Earline said you wanted."

"Like Earline said I wanted? Studying what?"

"This pamphlet." I held it out. "Earline said you wanted me to learn to take orders from her. So we could all act in concert on the trip. She said you told her she could punish me and this was a test to see if I could take orders."

He rubbed his forehead with his thumb. "I'm afraid Earline is acting out some dreadful sort of game with you, CeCe. I was afraid of something like this. You see, on the plantation she came from she had a mistress your age and the girl frequently had her beaten."

"Oh."

"I'm afraid it won't work with you two on the trip."

"You mean I can't go?"

He sighed. "I'll have a talk with her. But even if I do, can you take her going off into a fearful act once in a while?"

I shrugged. "As long as you're there."

"I'll be there. And I'll protect you. But you must co-operate. And try with her."

"I will, Uncle Alex. Just please let me go."

"You didn't want to go in the beginning. What changed your mind?"

Getting to know you, I wanted to say. Hearing about it at supper last night. Seeing how gentle you can be. And caring. "Seeing all this," I said.

He cleared his throat. "Which brings me to all this. Nobody is allowed in here. So, to my original question, young lady. *What are you doing in here?*"

"I told her to go into your surgery and study." It was Earline in the doorway. "I never told her to come in here."

"You said studio," I shot back.

"Do you think I'm daft? I know him longer than you. I know he doesn't allow anyone in here. Why would I—"

"You said *studio!*"

"I never did!" she shouted back.

"You stinking liar!" I yelled at her.

"CeCe!" Uncle Alex's voice rang out like a crack from Papa's whip. "Don't you *ever* talk like that in front of me again! Now say you're sorry."

I started to sob. I started toward him, arms outreached.

"No"—he turned away—"not until you do as I say."

"She lied about me." I hiccuped.

"I know what she did. She isn't my niece. You are."

So I said I was sorry to Earline. And Uncle Alex welcomed me into his arms.

"I'm not going to punish you, CeCe," he said, "as long as you tell me what you learned from that pamphlet. Earline, go about your business. You don't have to hear this."

She left in a huff.

"What do you want to know?" I asked.

"Tell me about the North Star. I love to hear about the North Star."

I recited. "The slaves who escaped liked to travel at night, especially nights when there was a North Star. They used it as their pilot. Many slaveholders hated the North Star and said that if they could they would rip it out of its place in the heavens."

"Good," he said quietly. "Very good. I'll ask you more questions about the pamphlet another time. I do believe there're enough hours left in the day for you to take Pelican for a nice jaunt."

"Thank you, Uncle," I said.

"For what?"

"For believing the reason I was in here."

He squeezed me. He turned me around and gave me a gentle pat on the head. "Go on with you," he said.

Chapter Six

UNCLE HAD trails that went through his woods, and the woods were alive with the likes of squirrels and rabbits and birds and wild turkeys. "Don't go beyond the pond," he'd said. So I didn't. Pelican and I rested as we got to the pond. I sat in a patch of sunlight that filtered down through the leaves of the trees as Pelican quietly grazed nearby. The pond was full of ducks, swimming around and enjoying themselves, ducking their heads underwater for whatever was there. I got up to watch one in particular, tripped over a root, twisted my ankle, and fell to the ground.

"Oh damn." I seldom cussed, but there was no other word to cover it. My ankle burned, but I made myself get up and mount Pelican, who, sensing something was wrong, seemed extra careful not to jog but kept at a smooth gait.

On the way home I noticed I was being followed by a wild turkey. He ducked in and out of the foliage, ran to catch up to me, opened both wings, and fanned his sides. Then he took two or three leaps in the air, shook himself, and began the whole business of following all over again.

I pretended I didn't see him. *He'll disappear when I get to the clearing in front of Uncle's house, if I ever get there,* I told myself. But he didn't. He followed me right around to the barn in back, doing his strange dance all the way. I dismounted and he rolled himself in the dust, as at home as I was. Then, in considerable pain, I started to unsaddle Pelican but couldn't, and ended up leaning against him instead.

Someone lifted the saddle from my hands.

It was Charlie, Uncle's man-with-the-horses. I stepped aside, leaning on the fence, and watched as he vigorously brushed Pelican down. The turkey flitted in and out of the barn. My ankle screamed in pain, but I was determined to let no one know I'd hurt it. We were leaving on our trip in two days.

Charlie came over with a fistful of corn and poured it into my hand. "Give it to Horace," he directed.

"Horace?"

"The turkey."

I poured it on the ground. Horace nibbled gratefully while I tried to figure out how I was going to get from the barnyard along the brick path into the back door of the house.

And then Uncle Alex came out, striding down the brick walk. "I see you found Horace. Or he found you."

"He followed me home, Uncle Alex. Is he one of your birds?"

"You could say that. I found him in the woods one day, one wing injured. I brought him home and nursed him. Then when he was better, I let him go. Days he spends in the woods, but nights he always comes home and roosts either in that tree over there or on my roof."

"Why does he come home?"

"I feed him. He wants to be close to me."

He was looking at me, half scowling. "Why are you favoring one foot, CeCe?"

"I'm not."

"Lie to someone who's not a doctor. I think you've got one wing injured, too. Walk on over to me, won't you?"

I was caught as if in a leg trap. I tried to walk natural-like but failed. I limped badly. I felt like Horace must have felt. And then my right leg gave way and I fell down.

He was at me in a minute, lifting me and carrying me

along the brick walk, into the house. Nancy opened the door.

"Told you that child isn't as big as her name, and sure enough not big enough to go riding off into the woods alone," she scolded him. "What kind of guardian are you?"

He took her scolding. Apparently she did it often. She opened the door to his surgery and he sat me down on the table, flipped up my skirt and petticoat, and started to unlace my boot. Only it wouldn't unlace. My ankle was too swollen. I cried out when he tried. From somewhere in the house came the sound of Aunt Elise playing the piano.

Out of his back pocket he took a knife. "What are you going to do?" I wailed.

"Don't you worry now, honey." Nancy held my hand. "He knows what he's about. He's the best doctor within a hundred miles. Did you know that when he goes on trips people don't want to go to Dr. Williams instead?"

Then why is he painting birds? I wanted to know. But I didn't say it.

Carefully, he cut at the boot, so carefully that he didn't even cut into the lace-trimmed ruffle of my pantalets or my hose, though the boot was ruined for good. Right down the side he cut it, then he pulled it off.

My ankle had swelled to twice its size. I started to cry.

"Undo the hose, Nancy," he directed.

I was grateful that he asked her to do it, glad that he wasn't going to go fishing, himself, under my skirts. And the fact that he respected my privacy was fixed in my memory. This was a man of good parts, as Aunt Susan Elizabeth would say. No doubt if I was run over by a carriage and was bloody all over and he had to rip off my clothes, he would. But he didn't have to now, so he treated me with decency.

I was getting to know him more and more. And the more I learned, the more I admired him, it seemed. How could that be? I had never admired Papa.

Apparently Nancy was his nurse. She reached under my skirts and undid the hose on that leg and drew it off while he was fetching bandages. Within no time at all he had the ankle wrapped tightly and was handing me a powder and water.

Then he lifted me off the table and carried me into the front parlor where Aunt Elise was playing the piano. He sat me down most carefully on the couch, against the pillows in the waning sun, and Nancy covered me with a throw.

"Don't move," he admonished. "That powder will soon start to take effect."

Aunt Elise stopped playing. "What happened?"

"She'll be all right in a day or two," he told her. "Sprained her ankle. Keep an eye on her, honey. She's likely to doze off."

"Oh, CeCe. Well, if your uncle Alex attended to you, you'll soon be well."

She sighed and looked down at her own legs and the thought hung over us all like a shadow. *But he'd attended her, and she wasn't well, was she?*

They looked at each other and he squeezed her hand. "We'll have to change our plans," he said.

"Please don't say I can't go," I begged.

"I was beginning to think that horseback wasn't such a good idea after all," he told us. "We'll go the other way. Packet boat or steamship. Whatever we can manage. Stagecoach. I've some arrangements to make now. Couriers to send with letters. You just get well."

TWO DAYS LATER we were packed but still hadn't left. Uncle Alex wanted to give me more time to recover. I was taking a walk around the house at the end of the day, because Uncle Alex said I should exercise a little, when Earline came up to me.

"Because of you, I won't be taking my eight-hundred-mile ride on horseback. And it was part of my paper I was going to write."

"I'm sorry," I said.

"You're not. You're getting all his attention. That's all you want."

I hadn't known it was eight hundred miles, and I was almost glad to spare Pelican. Charlie had promised to care for him while I was gone.

"Now we have to bring dresses to wear on the packet. I, of course, will wear dun-colored muslin. You will have fancy clothes and eat with the captain and have ice cream frozen with ice from New England ponds."

"You wanted to play the part of a slave."

"Let's not discuss that again. Why are you out here?"

"I'm waiting for somebody."

"Who?"

"Horace."

"Oh, that silly bird."

"Uncle saved him."

"Your uncle has killed as many birds as he's saved."

I just stared at her. "That's a lie."

"How do you think he paints them? Do you think they sit there and pose for him? Are you that much of a child? He once put a sharp knife through the heart of a golden eagle. He's a doctor. He knows what will kill them. Then he perched him on a branch and painted him. It took him about sixty hours. Didn't you see the painting in his studio?"

I had. I felt my face pale.

"Other times he shoots them. Ask him, why don't you. Sometimes he ships bird skins to England."

"Go away, please, and leave me be."

She smiled and raised her chin. Her slanted eyes shone with pride. "We'll see who is most help to him on this trip," she said. Then she turned to walk away, but stopped. "Oh, and someday ask him, why don't you, how his little son died. And how his wife became crippled."

"I know how," I said. "I know the story."

"All because of a bird," she emphasized. "No, perhaps you'd best not ask him. Just be mindful of it, and you won't think him such a hero."

I just stared at her. Then I said something I shouldn't have said. "That mistress of yours must have had you beaten once too often for you to hate me so," I said.

Before I knew what happened, she slapped my face.

I gasped. I reeled backward, almost fell, and caught myself. As I did I saw, over her shoulder, Uncle Alex standing on the front porch watching.

I put my hand to my face. "You impudent child," she said. "You're the one who deserves to be whipped." And she turned and walked up onto the front porch where Uncle Alex stopped her, and I heard them talking for a minute.

For just a second or two his voice was raised. "I will not have it," I heard. "One more instance and you will not go as my assistant. I'll manage without one. That child is not to be hit. By anyone."

She made a reply, a low murmur, a humble one. Then she went into the house.

He came down the porch steps and across the lawn to me. "How are you, CeCe?"

"I'm all right, Uncle."

He touched my face where she had slapped me. It hurt. "You ought to go in the house right now and have Nancy put a cold cloth on that face. Have yourself a nice calming cup of tea and then come into my studio. We have to talk."

"You mean your study, don't you, sir?"

"I said what I mean, CeCe. My studio. I'll wait for you there. Here, let me help you up to the porch."

I did as he said, then made my way upstairs. To be invited to his studio was an honor. And he was waiting for me at his desk.

I stood for a moment and stared, seeing things I hadn't seen the last time I was in here, like the empty birds' eggs, strung out with string running through them and pinned up on one wall. The painting of the common barn owl and that of the purple martin. And, of course, the golden eagle who'd had the knife put through his heart.

He patted a nearby chair, gesturing that I should sit. I did so.

"You're going to have to do me a favor sometime in the future," he said.

"Yes, Uncle."

"You're going to have to ask Earline about her experience on the plantation and how she ran away. Let her tell you her story. Will you do that for me?"

I ran my tongue along my lips. "Yes, sir. Am I still going with you then?"

"Of course you are. I've engaged a boat to take us to a steamer down the Ohio. Thereafter we'll go by steamer, stage, or mail coach if we have to. I'm accustomed to traveling, child. And I take the long way to see as many birds as I can see. And I promise you an adventure. But before we go, what has Earline been telling you about me?"

"It's nothing, Uncle."

"Come now, don't waste my time. Rumors swirl all around about me. Now I order you to tell me."

I hesitated, then spoke. "Earline says you shoot birds. She says that golden eagle up there . . ." I hesitated.

"Had a knife put through his heart? Yes, it's true. He

was a stout fellow. He died well. I respect him. Well, of course I shoot birds. How else could I paint them?"

He shook his head and smiled grimly. "She's a great assistant, that girl, but she's trying to turn you against me. We have a real female problem here I see. Did she tell you yet the one about how I overturned the carriage because I was looking at a bird and my little boy was killed and my wife crippled for life?"

I lowered my eyes.

"Well, did she? I will have an answer."

"Yes, sir."

"I'm not thirty yet and already I'm a legend, CeCe," he said. "You can believe that story if you want. Lots of people believe it. I'm beyond caring."

I sensed that he wanted to talk about it. "Tell me what really happened, Uncle Alex."

He raised his eyebrows and then he told me. "It was December and we were coming home from a Christmas party. The road was getting icier by the minute. The horse slipped. The carriage went over. The rest is . . . true. Except that I was thrown, too. I broke a leg. There was no bird, CeCe. There never was a damned bird. Now you can believe whatever you want, child. I'd give that broken leg if it had never happened."

I said nothing. I didn't have to. But it came to me then that he hadn't worked on Aunt Elise. He couldn't have. Not if his leg was broken. Had it been the good Dr. Williams? Is that why she could never walk again?

"Any more questions?" he asked.

I looked at the strung eggs on the wall. "How do you get the eggs out of the shells?" I asked him.

He got up and stood over me, his hand on my head, like a blessing. "You're an unusual child, CeCe," he said. "A lot like me. They can knock you down but they can't keep you there. Now, since I'm baring my soul, I've got something else to tell you, something that may really turn you against me and make you not want to come on the trip. Are you ready for it?"

"Yes, sir," I said.

He went to the window and looked out. "When I visit the plantations down South, I hunt for birds, yes. I go out into the fields and woods and spend the day. Evenings and mornings I dine at the tables of the plantation owners. Do you know what I do in return for their kindnesses?"

I shook my head no.

"I make it my business to circulate amongst the slaves. And when I do, I talk to them. I offer them advice on how to escape. I map out their route north and tell them where the safe houses are. It's how I met Earline. Sometimes I give the slaves small sums of money for their trips." He turned now to look at me.

"There. That's it. Now you can make up your mind if you still want to come along. If you do, you are sworn to secrecy because if I'm found out I'll likely be tarred and feathered. Maybe hanged or shot. You're under no obligation to do anything to help me if you come. You just act as yourself, my niece and my ward. If you don't want to come, that's all right, too."

I drew in my breath and looked at him, all of him, for the first time. He was tall, much taller than Papa, and slender. Last week some company had come over and three young girls in the crowd had giggled over his "handsomeness." Why did I not appreciate it? Because he was my uncle? I tried to see it now. He had icy blue eyes that laughed when he was happy and pierced you when he was angry. His hair was light brown and curly. His shoulders were broad and he was nothing if not gentle and refined and mannerly. Last week I had seen him bow to women, even kiss their hands. The girls had said that women all over were bedazzled by him. Aunt Elise had told me that he could fence and dance and speak French and Spanish.

It came to me that I, who had never looked up to any man, who had only feared Papa and never expected affection, was now starting to do something I never thought I would do. I was starting to see a man as someone to hold affection for. I was starting to love him and see him as a protector.

And now, here he was, placing himself in danger.

"Suppose you get killed," I said, "like my father?"

"I promise you I won't get killed. I've done this before. I've learned to charm the plantation owners to death, so they never suspect me of anything."

"Well," I said, "I'm going."

"Because you believe suddenly in what I'm doing?"

"No. Because you may need me."

An odd look came over his face, half quizzical and half embarrassed. "Am I to hope, within reason, that you might be coming to care for your crazy old uncle, CeCe?"

"You're not crazy and you're not old."

"That doesn't answer the question."

I got up and threw my arms around his waist, and he hugged me.

"That," he said, "answers the question."

Chapter Seven

WE MADE our trip just as Uncle Alex said we would. From a flatboat on the Ohio, to a packet to a steamer. From river to river. Somewhere in between there was a stagecoach. I do not recollect much because I made a disgrace of myself.

I was seasick on both the packet boat and the steamer. And the bumping and rocking of the stagecoach didn't help my sorry state at all.

From my berth on the steamship, I could hear the hooting of the great owl and the muffled sound of its wings as it sailed over the steam. Oh, how I wished I had the strength to be on deck so I could see it. And I could hear the boatmen's horns, acknowledging us from other vessels, through the fog. Like we were traveling through an eerie fairy tale.

Birdsong by day and by night fiddles playing on the decks and the sounds of dancing. I was missing it all.

Somewhere in my misery I knew that we were traveling down the Ohio.

I knew, because as Uncle was holding my head over the basin while I was throwing up or having the dry heaves, he was coolly telling me so. Telling me gently about the scenery outside, while wiping my forehead with cloths soaked in vinegar or giving me cold tea with which to wash my mouth out.

In time, my stomach adjusted to the rocking of the water and I was able to move about and go on deck. Ah, the fresh air was a welcome respite from my stagnant cabin.

THE CAPTAIN, whose wife Uncle had done a portrait of onboard, had given Earline and me a cabin in the stable center of the ship and Uncle Alex an amidship stateroom. The steamer had a ladies' parlor, a bathhouse, and when I could finally eat at the table, I tasted that ice cream kept cool with ice from the ponds of New England, as Earline had predicted.

I joined Uncle Alex the evening he dined with the captain. I wore my pink dress with the ruffles on the skirt and the wide collar, anxious to make up to Uncle for my sickness. I was on my best behavior. I knew he wanted to show me off. His niece. His ward. He puffed up with pride.

After I'd had my dinner and my treat, my ice cream, and it was time for the men to have their liquor, I was dismissed and allowed to go to the ladies' parlor. Earline was in the doorway of the dining room waiting for me.

"A sweet child," I heard the captain say as I walked away. "And such a pretty little thing. There's an innocence about her that . . . well, you're very fortunate, Doctor."

"Yes, I am," Uncle agreed. "After we lost our son, my wife and I thought there was no chance for us to ever raise another child again."

Earline had been playing the part of my servant (or slave) since we started the trip. She wore plain muslin and cotton with a turban around her head and a snow-white apron at all times.

And from the time she helped Uncle Alex carry his supplies aboard, she spoke with a slave accent, bowing and humbling herself. There were many supplies, but Uncle Alex carried the heavier ones.

Besides his gun he had a wooden box with a small stock of linen, drawing paper, his journal, colors and pencils, twenty-five pounds of shot, some flints, cotton with which to stuff birds, cash, and "a heart true to nature," he said.

I had personally watched him pack the wooden box, fascinated. From all this came those pictures of birds?

At Louisville the steamer dropped anchor. Oh we stopped before, at many places along the way, at farmlands to take on fresh butter and milk and perishables. Uncle insisted I sit out on deck in the fresh air when the nausea abated, and I saw the young country folk come aboard selling things. Quilts, apples, honey, freshly baked bread.

In Louisville, Kentucky—a deep slave state, Uncle explained—we took rooms at the Indian Queen Hotel. Uncle told the innkeeper that Earline had to be in the room with me. She was my "servant" and I had been seasick and was still not well. So we roomed together. But we didn't dine together. In the Indian Queen Hotel I would have to eat alone in the dining room rather than have a negro sit at the table with me. Earline ate in the kitchen with the other servants. Three meals a day.

Uncle instructed that I write a letter to Aunt Elise, telling her that I was well again. And another to Aunt Susan Elizabeth. We could get the letters in the mail pouches of ships going north. He was writing, he said, to his agent in Philadelphia.

"And when did you write to Aunt Susan Elizabeth last?"

"Two weeks ago," I lied.

I still lie to him on occasion. I don't know why. I still have the habit of lying, afraid of being punished, afraid of being beaten, like my father would do, though I know Uncle Alex never would. It isn't his way. But I lie and hate myself for it.

He's so honest with me, so gentle and so decent that I live in fear he'll find out I'm lying. Then what would I do? I'd have to run away, into the woods like Horace the wild turkey. I'd have to roost in the trees.

I wrote the letters. We stayed three days in Louisville. And I finally got to ask Earline about her life as a slave.

WE WERE IN the ladies' sitting room of the hotel. It was after Uncle and I had dined and I was starting to cough from the cigar smoke in the dining room.

"Going to the Boot Room," he said. "You'd best go to the ladies' parlor. Get away from this smoke. Earline should be waiting there for you. I gave her instructions."

He got up and pulled out my chair. I knew the Boot Room was where they served liquor and played cards.

He kissed me. "Bed by nine. Remember you're still not completely well."

"Yes, sir."

"You look nice tonight." He pulled a strand of my hair, teasing. "When we get to Savannah I'm going to have two new dresses made for you at Messrs. Habersham and Son."

"YOU WANT to know *what*?" Earline could not believe what I was asking.

"About your life back at the plantation and how you escaped. How Uncle Alex helped you."

We were alone in the ladies' parlor. "Why?"

"Uncle thinks it will help me understand you better."

"And you? What do you think? Do you even care to think?"

I sighed. "I'd like to know what makes you dislike me, so, yes, Earline. I don't know anything about slavery."

"But they came to your father's house. He took them in. He saved them. And you never bothered to speak to them?"

"No."

"Why?"

"I didn't want my father endangering his life. Or getting in trouble for people he didn't even know."

"You loved him that much."

"No. I hated him."

"Why?"

"He beat me. He said I had no soul. He hated me."

She fell silent. "Why did he hate you so? Did you ever ask him?"

"You didn't do that with my father."

"Then why don't you ask your uncle. He knows everything."

I had never thought of that.

"Very well, I'll answer your question," she said. "But in return you must do something for me."

"What?"

"You're going to have to start ordering me about. It's what you always wanted to do, isn't it?"

I shook my head no. "I never wanted—"

"Oh, don't bother lying. You don't do lying well. If you don't learn to order me about, we're all going to get caught out on the plantations. You must talk firmly to me. And don't bother being nice. Call me dense once in a while. Or lazy. Lazy is one of their favorite words. And if I don't please you, you must slap me. On the face, on the arm, anywhere. Are you listening, CeCe?"

"How can I do that?" I asked. *That's the way I was treated by my father.*

"You must. Or your uncle will be in trouble. Just be mean. Well? Order me to do something!"

Just then the door opened and a handsome-looking woman came in. I'd seen her on the steamer. Immediately Earline stood up.

The woman wore a crimson frock with puffed sleeves and a fur-trimmed shawl. "My, it's cold. My name is Mrs. Abraham. And you. You must be the daughter of that handsome Dr. McGill. I saw you dining together this evening. How are you, child? Enjoying the trip?"

I stood up and curtsied, as I'd been taught by Aunt Susan Elizabeth. "I'm his niece, ma'am. My name is Cecelia, but everybody calls me CeCe."

"He's an artist, too, isn't he, your uncle?"

"Yes, ma'am."

"I saw the portrait he did of the captain's wife when we were on the ship."

"Mostly he draws birds."

"Oh, so he's *that* Dr. McGill."

"Yes, ma'am."

"I've heard of him. He gets invited to plantations, and he scouts out birds that haven't been identified before and paints them. Am I correct?"

"Yes, ma'am."

"Where is he headed now? May I ask?"

I saw no harm in telling. "Georgia, ma'am."

"I suppose he's got a whole list of invitations."

"No, ma'am. He hasn't any." I looked at Earline. "Am I right?"

"Thas' right, miss," she said in a Southern accent I hadn't heard from her before. "We'alls goin' to jus' play it by ear, ma'am," she told Mrs. Abraham.

The woman seemed annoyed to be addressed by a slave. "And you are?" she asked.

"This is Earline, my girl," I said. "She serves me and accompanies me everywhere. Has since I was a knee baby. But she also assists Uncle with his supplies. She carries things and fetches for him. If he shoots a bird, for instance, she brings it back. At home his dog does this for him, but he couldn't bring his dog along on the trip."

The woman smiled, liking the comparison of Earline to a dog. "Well, if you all don't have a place to start off your expedition, you must come to Greenbriar, our plantation near Greensburg, not far from Savannah. He will find all the woods and fields he wants for his scouting, and the place abounds in springs and rivulets. I shall invite him. Where is he tonight?"

"In the Boot Room, ma'am."

"Very well, I shall have your girl take a note in to him. Can you spare her for a few moments?"

"Of course," I said.

She reached into a small satchel that she was carrying and took out paper and pencil and wrote the note, all the while talking. "I'm traveling alone. My servant is making up my bed. I shall retire early tonight. I was visiting my sister in Tennessee. Here." And she reached out, note in hand. "What is your name? Geraldine?"

Earline gave a small curtsy. "Earline, ma'am."

"Well, bring this to Dr. McGill, please. I'll await his reply."

"And bring back a tray of tea and small cakes, Earline." I surprised myself giving orders. "Don't lollygag as you usually do or I'll slap you good. You hear?"

Earline dragged her feet and swished out of the room. "Yes, miss. I'm a-goin'."

And she went.

"And don't you dare stop and talk to anyone, either," I called after her. "Or I'll tell Dr. McGill and he'll punish you good."

I surprised myself. *I don't even need lessons,* I thought. *I'm good at this.* Then I was frightened. It was easy, too easy. Is this how simple it was for people in the South? How ordinary? And tempting to do every day?

Aunt Susan Elizabeth used to say there was something in all of us that delighted in bullying those lower in the social order of things. And that was what made slavery so easy for the white folks to practice.

My father said fear is what made it easy to practice. That down in the Deep South there were places where the blacks outnumbered the whites. And the whites had to keep them under control.

Both reasons frightened me. Because whatever my reason was, I was good at it.

Chapter Eight

"I DON'T KNOW how I can abide having a young mistress. I ran away from one," Earline said as I came into our room that night.

She had my basin of warm water ready for my washing, my bed turned back, my nightclothes out. She was looking after me, not just playing the part. I supposed I should be grateful, but I was getting confused. Which was the real Earline? The one caring for me now or the one pretending to be my slave?

I feared I would make a mistake and mix them up and say something to give Uncle's secret away.

Now she was looking hurt. Downstairs in the ladies' parlor I had slapped her.

It was when she came back with the tray of tea. She had forgotten the small cakes. Was it on purpose? Was she inviting trouble? Had she done it to convince Mrs. Abraham she was just a dense, lazy slave and not an Oberlin student?

I hadn't wanted to slap her. Honestly. But then she sassed me, too. And I had no choice.

She'd just handed the note from Uncle Alex to Mrs. Abraham and set the tray down. I saw there were no cakes and asked where they were.

She rolled her eyes. "Oh, I suppose I forgot 'em."

"Well, you lazy girl. I told you not to."

"It's all right, CeCe," Mrs. Abraham said.

"No, it isn't," I said. "She's done it just to plague me. Now go and get them, Earline. And be quick about it."

Her eyes went over me. "You'd be better off wifout 'em, I 'spect," she said.

It was then that I slapped her face, much as she had done to me back home. "Now go up to our room," I said. "And prepare it for my bedtime. You can be sure Uncle is going to hear about this."

Now, in our room, I asked if I'd hurt her.

"I had it coming," she said.

She helped me out of my dress and I washed myself. I didn't want to go to the women's bathhouse. You sometimes had to wait in line. I'd wake up early tomorrow when the others slept and bathe myself. I put on my nightgown and hopped into bed.

"Now tell me what it was like for you and how you ran away," I said.

"Your uncle said in bed by nine."

"I am in bed."

She shook her head. "You do try that good man sometimes. All right. The plantation I come from was in Wheeling, Virginia. My master had two hundred slaves. Tobacco land. But I worked in the house. I was"—here she sighed—"you won't believe this, but I was the 'girl' to a little spoiled miss the age you are now. That's what makes this thing so frightfully scary. I was her age. Brought into the house to cater to her every whim, fetch for her, play with her, pick up after she made messes, get scolded when she made mistakes, even spanked when I 'allowed' her to do something bad.

"When I grew to about fourteen, her daddy, Master Ballantine, started looking at me in a way that I didn't like. I stayed away from him much as I could. She saw this, of course, saw her father leering at me. She blamed me and started having me whipped for the slightest infraction. She'd stand by and watch.

"Then one day your uncle came to visit and to look for his birds.

"I was at supper in the quarters with a handful of the slaves, where I was allowed to eat once a week with my mama. He came in to say hello. There were five women all together. And me. He started talking to us. About escaping. And safe houses. He told us how the Ohio River was only fifty yards wide near Wheeling, and if we waited until winter it would freeze and we could walk across to Ohio and freedom.

"He gave us some money. Even me. I remember the way he looked at me. I had marks on my arms and legs from being whipped, and he took me aside and took some concoction out of his doctor's bag and put it on my scars. He got me talking. I told him about Master Ballantine. He advised me not to wait until winter."

She paused, remembering. "Could I swim? he asked. I said yes. He said that because we were having a drought the river was low right now. That I should swim across. Tell nobody. That his house was a safe house in Ripley, right on the river in Ohio. He told me how to get there. And that if there were lights in every window and his wife's quilt out on the fence in front, it was safe to come on in. And then he left.

"Well, I lay awake all that night thinking on it. I knew I didn't have a fancy for any more whippings. Or for Master Ballantine's advances. And neither did I want any more slaps or mouth from my mistress. But I also knew that if I left, likely I'd never see my mama again. And I couldn't even tell her I was leaving or she'd try to stop me.

"But two nights later I slipped out of my bed and out of the big house and made my way down to the river with just the money Dr. Alex had given me and the clothes on my back.

"Oh I was scared, for sure. Those dogs in the pens barked. But I walked across a stream like Dr. Alex had told me so the dogs couldn't pick up my scent. I walked the seven or eight miles down to the bend in the river where it was only fifty yards across. And then I waded out. And I swam across. Lucky for me there was a half-moon. And it was a clear night so I followed the North Star."

The North Star, I thought, remembering how Uncle Alex loved hearing about it.

"It was easy," she said. "Even if I didn't have the sense God gave a cocklebur, I could have followed Dr. Alex's directions on the other side. I was exhausted, of course, and hungry and cold, even though it was July, but I saw the lights in every window of his house, and sure enough there was that quilt on the fence, so I knew it was all right to climb those steps going up the bluff and knock, bold as brass, on his front door."

"And, so," I asked, "did you?"

"Yes. And I felt like I was walking up to heaven."

"Couldn't your master have come after you?"

"I fled before the Fugitive Slave Act," she said. "Before he had the right to come and get me and bring me back."

"So what did Uncle Alex do with you?"

"He took me into his surgery and looked me over. Nancy was there. I started crying of a sudden and she quieted me down. She took me in hand and bathed me and dressed me in warm clothes and gave me something to eat and bedded me down. And the next day Dr. Alex made arrangements for me to be taken to Canada to friends of his. I was educated in Canada. When I came back I was eighteen and grown, and he got me into Oberlin."

"Couldn't you still get caught?"

"I've grown up so and changed in appearance, and in my manner of speech. If Master Ballantine tripped over me he wouldn't recognize me today. Anyway, when we go to Georgia, your uncle has forged papers that I am his bonded slave. He paid fifteen hundred dollars for me."

Then she gave the conversation another turn. "When you slapped me downstairs. Was that in return for when I slapped you back home?"

"No," I said. "I was pretending."

"You're doing well with pretending," she replied.

WE DEPARTED Louisville the next morning. Uncle Alex had accepted Mrs. Abraham's invitation to visit her plantation first, and so she availed herself of his company for the rest of the trip. He escorted her around. He pointed out to her the scenery, the plantations along the river, the level plains, the swampy areas, the peach orchards, the sawmills, and the lumber floating down the river to market.

She should have been pointing it out to him, I decided, but she was playing at being coy, the Southern belle. Uncle knew how to deal with her, playing his hand to the hilt without falling under her spell.

"How is it that she's flirting with you when she has a husband?" I asked him in private at breakfast when she slept late.

"All Southern women flirt," he told me. "It's their way of conducting themselves with men. You'd do well to watch her. Learn some fine points of manners."

"Do you want me to be like that?"

He smiled ruefully and tugged at my earlobe. "I'd just as soon you had Choctaw blood in you than be like that," he said.

"Earline and I had a chance to practice our slave and mistress act in front of her the other night."

"I heard about it. Heard all about how you slapped Earline."

"And what do you think of it?"

"I'd say you were taking it rather far."

I sipped my morning tea. "Uncle, there's something real bad I have to tell you."

"Is it going to ruin my breakfast?"

"I hope not."

He sighed. "Go ahead."

"I *enjoyed* calling Earline names like stupid and dense. I enjoyed belittling her. Is that what it feels like to have slaves? Is that why Southerners do it?"

"They do it for economic reasons, CeCe. But I'm sure they enjoy it, too."

"What does that make me?"

"A little girl getting even for how she's treated you. I was hoping this wouldn't happen. Did she tell you the story of why she ran away?"

"Yes, sir."

"And you still don't feel any sympathy or kindness for her?"

I shrugged. "A little, I suppose."

"Well, suppose you nurture that little into more. Do you know that she had a child in Canada?"

I blinked at him. I stared at him. Hard.

"I didn't think she'd tell you that. Master Ballantine had attacked her. She told me about it when we met, and that's why I advised her not to wait until winter to escape. When she came to me she was already pregnant.

She had the baby in Canada and left him there with friends. They write to her on occasion to let her know how he's doing. You've had an unhappy childhood, though not like hers by half. So I thought you could empathize a bit. Is that too much to ask?"

The waitress poured me more tea and him more coffee. I waited until she left. "I'll try, Uncle."

"Yes. You do that. And I want no more slapping. On either side. The day may come, in this experiment of ours, when you have to defend each other. Do you understand me?"

He was not angry; he was serious, concerned, worried. He was solemn, grave.

I said yes, sir. I did.

Chapter Nine

WHEN WE disembarked in Savannah and stood on the dock that morning, we had to wait for Earline and Deliah, Mrs. Abraham's maid, to come up from steerage, where they had taken their breakfast.

"Sorry to be late, massa," Earline said as she picked up most of his supplies, which were packed in canvas. He carried his own portmanteau and gun, also wrapped in canvas, his cork-lined box with some of his paintings, and his wooden box with his art supplies. Earline carried her bag of clothing and I carried my portmanteaus.

The first impression I got of Georgia was the heat. It hit me in the face as we stood there on that dock. I had never in all my days felt such heat. It was not to be borne. It was a living, crawling thing, set out to smother you. Didn't anybody else notice but me?

"What's wrong, CeCe?" Uncle asked.

"The heat," I managed to say without seeming hysterical.

"Oh, that. You'll get used to it," Mrs. Abraham said.

Used to it? I looked around me on the wharf. What I saw were half-naked black men unloading the ships and women with veiled faces being hurried into carriages. And there was another thing.

Their faces were veiled because of the bugs. Now I was no sissy-boots, but it seemed like the bugs were trying to get into my ears and nose and winning.

"There are four hotels," Mrs. Abraham said. "The Pulaski House is the best." She put on her hat with the veil over her face.

"Then the Pulaski House it is," Uncle Alex said.

We were staying for two nights. Uncle had business at the Exchange, and then was keeping his promise to have two new dresses made for me.

"I want a veiled hat, too," I told him.

"We've already got one for you," he said. "It's packed away."

Mrs. Abraham had calls to make. Uncle hailed a carriage, and as we drove along the street they called the Bay, according to Mrs. Abraham's chatter, I could not but be taken with the masts of all the ships at the wharves that were loading with cotton, at the brick streets themselves, at the trees that lined them, the laurel, the myrtle, the magnolia. Along the Bay were the counting-houses, the warehouses, the best shops, the post office, and the Exchange.

"Cotton is sixty cents a pound in Augusta," Uncle Alex said. "I understand it's the first thing I'm going to be asked when I shake hands with someone."

"Absolutely," Mrs. Abraham said. "And the size of their daughter's wedding or whether or not they can send their son off to Princeton depends on that price."

"Look, Uncle Alex, there's a bookseller. Can you take me there tomorrow, please?" I begged.

"Of course, CeCe."

I listened as Mrs. Abraham told Uncle Alex that Savannah had ten thousand people and how five thousand of them were white. And how those white people worried about a slave uprising. How could she say such things in front of Earline and Deliah? She spoke in front of them as if they were not there.

Later Uncle Alex told me that was the way all Southerners treated their slaves. As if they were pieces of furniture. As if they were not there.

Our party of five cost ten dollars a day at the Pulaski. Uncle Alex insisted upon paying. Mrs. Abraham had her own room and so did I. Uncle Alex had his. Earline and Deliah had to sleep in the basement with the other slaves. I had noticed that Earline had a notepad and had already started making notes when in our presence. She gave the pad to Uncle Alex for safekeeping, lest anyone see that she could write.

He didn't read it. "They are her private thoughts," he told me. "She hasn't yet given me permission."

A man of good parts, I thought again.

The next day Uncle took me to Habersham and Son to have me fitted for two new dresses. I went into the back room to be fitted by a woman dressmaker, to have the fabric pinned and tucked and ruffled about me as Aunt Susan Elizabeth would do. And when it sufficiently resembled a dress, Uncle Alex was invited back for his approval.

He was very interested, very critical. And he looked at me as if I were one of his birds. He had an eye for beauty, being an artist, and he did make several suggestions. The dressmaker knew who he was and was anxious to please him. One dress was blue and one yellow, then for good measure he had two everyday calicos thrown in. I was growing, he said. "I hope in mind as well as body," he teased.

After that we went to the booksellers and he allowed me several books. He was interested here, also. No, he didn't insist on science or mathematics. He did, since he was responsible for my education, suggest one *Life of*

George Washington and one story about the Revolutionary War. I wanted romantic novels. "Please, Uncle?" I begged.

I was shameless. I batted my eyes in the Mrs. Abraham fashion. I tipped my head. He smiled. He knew what I was doing, but he liked it anyway.

"All right, two," he said, "but only if you buy one Shakespeare and one other book of poetry. Memorize some and recite it for me. Before you go off to school in the fall. If you decide to stay with me."

I agreed to the bargain. I was going off to the local village school in Ripley.

That afternoon when we went back to the Pulaski House, we found out about the party being given by the gentlemen who lived there. All the strangers who were staying were invited. There were a lot of military people there and Uncle said we could go.

For a change Earline was permitted to go with us, to attend to me, to hold my shawl and my fan when I was asked to dance by a young cadet who had come with a group from a local military academy. I thanked Aunt Susan Elizabeth again, for her insisting on my learning my manners, for her insisting I learn to dance and curtsy and make conversation.

Uncle said he was proud of me. Earline was proud because the whole of the band consisted of negroes. She could not stand still and jiggled as she listened to the music.

The next day we left for Greenbriar, Mrs. Abraham's plantation not far from Savannah.

The house was most appealing, and from the distant road, with the magnolias dripping over its columned front, with jessamine vine, *Camellia japonicas*, and oranges on trees, one couldn't help but admire it.

All but Uncle Alex gave a cry of "ohhh." His attention was drawn to sparrows chirping, the doves hopping about, and the mockingbirds whistling at us.

"You won't have to go far to find what you want here," Mrs. Abraham told him.

"Imagine what I will find if I *do* go far," he said.

I think Earline's cry was that of the pain of remembrance. Mine was the only one of admiration. The house, after all, was beautiful, with a peaked roof and a porch that reached up to the second story and a coolness that pervaded the place.

As the carriage drew up in front, half a dozen negroes came to see to their duties. They were all nicely dressed. Some house servants came out to greet us, too, and I noticed they were all mulatto, and dressed in the same spotless mode as the coach negroes.

They took our things. They looked Earline up and down and led her away with them. Mr. Abraham came out onto the porch and greeted us, kissed his wife, shook Uncle's hand, kissed mine, and invited us in.

In spite of the fact that we were in Georgia, the house was cool and the fire he had burning in the fireplace was welcome.

"My boys came back last night from a hunting party," he told us, "and brought a boatload of venison, fish, and fowl. We plan to have much of it for dinner tonight. And other delicacies to be found only on a rice plantation. Dr. McGill, our lands abound with articles of interest, not only to the game hunter but to the naturalist and artist. My plantation is yours to study."

His boys could not keep from staring at Earline as she helped serve Uncle Alex and me at supper. She was wearing the slaves' turban around her head, which only served to bring out the roundness of her face, the beauty of her slightly slanted eyes. She was garbed in her best calico. No rags for the slaves on this plantation.

Even Uncle Alex noticed how Mr. Abraham's boys couldn't take their eyes from her. And I saw his concern.

But others saw it, too. That very night, after Earline finished getting me ready for bed, the mulattoes, the house servants who lived in brick cabins adjoining the house and stables, were waiting for her outside my bedroom door.

"I'll see you in the morning," she said.

Normally in such a setting, she would sleep on a mattress outside my door. Not that I wanted her to, but this was the way of Southern plantations.

"Your uncle suggested I go with the house servants to their quarters. The sons, Raphael and John, are on the prowl." She took out from her apron pocket a small knife. "They think it is their right to have me this night. And I think it is my right to kill them, first. Uncle wants no trouble. And so I go to the house servants' quarters."

I nodded my good nights. In a minute, Uncle was there in the hall. I looked up at him. "Will they bother me?" I asked, tremulously.

"No. But if you're frightened, my room is next door. There's a dressing room in it. And a settee. I'll move it into the dressing room for you. Or you can sleep in here and lock your door."

I didn't want to be a baby, but I was afraid. Uncle saw it and nodded. He took me by the hand and into his room, where the dressing room was large enough for me to sleep. He moved the settee inside, and in no time I was comfortable and secure.

"Those boys are hellions," he said. "Give them to me one day and I'd have them straight. And they say the name 'abolitionist' hereabouts is more dangerous than the label incendiary, rebel, or murderer," he murmured.

Sure enough, that night when the clock in the downstairs hall struck two, I heard Uncle get up out of bed in his room and creep slowly toward the hall.

Next door, where I should have been sleeping, there was a rustling and stumbling about in my room. Some muffled laughter and some yelps.

In a minute I was out of bed and standing in the door of Uncle's room. I didn't dare go out into the hall. I didn't dare let him know I was listening. But I heard everything.

I heard him in my room, accosting Raphael and John, who were apparently looking for me.

"She's not *here*!" came the cry of disappointment.

"No, she isn't, is she?" came Uncle's voice. "You drunken, dissipated, lewd roustabouts!" Then I heard some severe slaps. And cries from the boys. "Mister, please, we were after the negro, not the little girl."

"You damn well were after the little girl. And that negro is mine. You harm her and I'll rip you apart." More slaps, this time harder. "I ought to whip you both within an inch of your life!"

"No, no, please, we're sorry, we wouldn't hurt the little girl, or the negro," they were saying.

"Get to bed. And you'd best be gone before breakfast tomorrow or I'll tell your father. Damned mongrels. Uncivilized beasts! Out to break your mother's heart!"

It was all over in a minute, the scuffling, the hitting, the noise. Soon the house was silent again, as if nothing had happened. I was back in bed when I heard Uncle come into his room, sit down on the bed, and pour himself a drink. I turned my head a bit and I could see the shaft of light from his lamp on the floor.

In a little while he got up and came into the dressing room and peered down at me. I pretended to be sleeping. He put his hand on my head briefly and then left and blew out his lamp and went back to bed.

The next day we set out on a hunting trip of our own.

THERE WAS no mention at breakfast of last night's doings. If Mr. and Mrs. Abraham suspected anything, they said nothing. All was bright and cheerful in the sun-filled dining room. Servants hovered. The aroma of good food filled the air. Mr. Abraham presided, proud as Horace, our strutting pet turkey.

The boys were off early on their hunting trip, he told us. Ahem. Industrious young men. Wouldn't be back for two days. Likely we wouldn't see them again. They tendered their good-byes.

We were off this morning, Uncle said. And he and Mr. Abraham discussed the plantation's yield, the rice, the corn, sweet potatoes, peanuts for the swine, and melons. And the number of slaves. Two hundred.

They talked about the price of rice, and in the next minute the price of a good field hand, the fledgling railroads in Georgia.

"I'd like, while you are here, for you to talk with Old Tom," Mr. Abraham said. "He's the son of a prince of the Foulah tribe. He was taken prisoner at fourteen near Timbuktu. He remembers plants and insects of Africa."

Uncle said yes, then asked how to get to the nearest swamp. Today he was looking for the ivory-billed woodpecker, he explained. "The swamp is his favorite resort. And I'm always looking for the Ever-After Bird. The slaves call him that," he explained. "His real name is the scarlet ibis. Might I talk to some of your slaves to see if they've seen it?"

Mr. Abraham agreed that it was all right.

I was sent to put on my trekking outfit. Aunt Elise had made it for me. It was a dun-colored skirt that was divided like pants and a tree-green cotton blouse with long sleeves and a cape for a collar to ward off the rain. And here was the wide-brimmed hat to keep the sun off my face. This morning I, and Earline and even Uncle, wore mosquito netting around our hats and down around our faces and necks so we wouldn't be bitten. I was to wear this outfit whenever I accompanied Uncle into the fields and forests and swamps. The divided skirt, tucked into boots, made it easier to climb over things, and the color made me part of the forests. Uncle had designed it for me, so I wore it happily that very day.

There was also a gray-colored haversack to carry my lunch and whatever else I needed. Earline carried her notebook and pencil in hers.

It was hot already when we set out on horseback, the ground all about was covered with mud and water. Bugs with large wings tormented me about the face, but the mosquito netting kept them from reaching my skin.

The swamp we visited was in the middle of the woods and the rice stalks all around were about five feet high and we had to maneuver our horses through them.

On the edges of the swamp we saw three or four slaves making canoes out of large cypress trees. They would sell them for four dollars apiece, they told Uncle.

They invited him to try one and so he did. He left his horse with us on the dry island, and I saw him talking with the slaves while in the canoe. Earline and I listened to the croaking of the frogs and watched out for the open mouths of alligators. I saw Uncle gesturing and pointing and saw the slaves listening intently.

I knew he was telling them about the Underground Railroad. About safe houses and routes north. Then I saw him pointing to the heavens and wondered if he was telling them about the North Star or asking about the Ever-After Bird.

Earline paid no mind. She just kept writing in that fool notebook of hers.

She wasn't even looking at the fairyland around us, the fallen and decaying trunks of trees, the dark cypresses protecting us from the sun with their dripping branches, the water lilies, the rich mosses that gleamed in the sun like green jewels.

Uncle had warned me, "Don't reach, don't touch, don't pick anything. Just sit on that log and wait for me. I don't want to fish you out of the water before an alligator gets you."

Birds whipped their wings overhead as they scurried from one tree to another. I looked for the scarlet ibis. Instead I saw the lesser scaup, the duck to be found in the rice fields about Savannah. Oh yes, I knew some birds by now. In my haversack I had a small book, given to me by Uncle, of sketches he'd done for me to learn from.

But no scarlet ibis. And no ivory-billed woodpecker.

Earline grinned at me. We were, whether we liked it or not, in competition with each other. A fierce competition to see who would first spot the scarlet ibis. When had it started? And how? Neither of us knew. All we knew was that we both wanted to be the first to point it out to Uncle, the first to spot it.

"You'll never see it. You're not quick enough. And if you see it first, you won't point it out to him," she said.

"And why is that?" I challenged.

"Because you know he'll pick up his gun and shoot it."

I felt my face pale. I said nothing.

"You haven't the courage," she pronounced. "It takes courage to assist him. Why you're just a simpering little girl. You're not even a woman yet, are you?"

I glowered at her now.

"Do you get your woman's time of the month?" she pushed.

I knew about it. Aunt Susan Elizabeth had prepared me. "No," I said.

"Well, see? You're almost fourteen. Why not? Did you ever wonder why? Because you're not enough of a woman is why. What do you know of blood and pain? How could you point out a beautiful bird for him to kill? Afterward he takes it and stuffs it, you know. Why do you think he brought along all that cotton? Then he paints it and ends up with something beautiful. It's like childbirth. First there's blood and pain, then there's something beautiful. Could you witness all that? I have."

Was she talking about her child now, or seeing Uncle stuff a bird? I dared not ask. I drew in my breath and looked across the swamp at Uncle Alex. He was giving something to the slaves. Money. They were nodding, and now he was directing them to bring him back to our island.

"My mother died when she had me," I told her.

"No, she didn't."

Her flying in the face of truth like that brought me up short. "Yes, she did. What do you know?"

"More than you. Because he told me."

I felt resentment, like a knife inside me. "And why not me?"

"Did you ask?"

I hadn't. But it was my business, my *private* business, not hers, and I was angry with Uncle for telling her. And I'd ask him soon. Maybe this afternoon.

On the way home he shot a female hooded merganser, a bird that frequented the rice fields and ponds, a nice bird with a long beak. A brown bird with feathers that stuck out in back making it look like a hood. He was all excited about it. He fetched it out of the water himself.

I insisted on watching him stuff it. He insisted I change first because my clothes were wet. He stuffed it out on the broad piazza in back. When I came down from changing, I asked him the questions that were bothering me.

Chapter Ten

I WALKED AROUND him first, watching, keeping my distance. His jacket was off, his sleeves were rolled up, and his hands and forearms were bloody.

Earline had said I could not witness blood. Well, I wasn't fainting, was I?

"Hand me those scissors, will you, CeCe? Where's Earline?"

"She's gone to clean up."

"You two were sitting too near the water this afternoon. Alligators have been known to grab little children who were too near the water. Earline knows better. I'll have to talk to her. What is it? Why are you circling me?"

"Uncle, I have a doctor question."

"I have to do this. I know you don't like the killing. Neither do I. Nobody respects nature more than I. But they aren't going to sit there and pose for me, CeCe, and I only shoot the ones I'm going to study and paint."

"No, it's about me."

He looked at me. "Are you ailing?"

"No, sir, but I need a question answered."

"Go on."

"Why haven't I had my woman's time of the month yet? I'll be fourteen come December. Earline says it's because I'm not enough of a woman to know about blood and pain. Is that true?"

He went on stuffing his bird. "Is Earline a doctor?"

"No, sir."

"Has no one else told you about this?"

"Aunt Susan Elizabeth told me some. But not enough."

He sighed heavily and went on working. "Well, every young lady comes to it in her own time. Some don't until they're sixteen. It has nothing to do with not being enough of a woman or not being able to know about blood or pain. I'd say, for all you've been through in your life, and from what I've observed about you, that you're enough of a young woman for anybody's liking, CeCe. Certainly for mine, and I have very high standards."

"Thank you, Uncle."

"Now is there anything else?"

"Yes, sir, I'm afraid there is."

Another heavy sigh. "Let's hear it then."

"I need to know how my mother died. Earline says she didn't die when she had me."

"Earline is just full of pleasant information these days, isn't she."

"Uncle, please, can you tell me? My father always said she died when she had me. He always hated me for that. Now what am I supposed to think?"

He was busily stuffing his bird. "The truth, CeCe, and it's a big truth. Your mother didn't die in childbirth. She lived two weeks after and was fine. I was living with your father at the time, so I know. He was away from the farm and she developed what they call childbed fever. I personally think it's a catchall phrase for any type of sickness a new mother gets, from my experience. Anyway, she needed a doctor. And they sent me across Two Horse Creek to fetch your father and his friend Dr. Griffin at Felicity York's house. I had orders from Aunt Susan Elizabeth: Bring them right home so they can see to your mama.

"Well, Felicity was sickly that week and your father wouldn't leave her. And he talked Dr. Griffin into not leaving her, either. He said she had cholera. She didn't."

"Then why did he . . ."

He looked at me with those blue eyes. "Your father and Felicity were smitten with each other, CeCe. You're enough of a woman to be told that now."

I nodded and swallowed. So that's what there was about Felicity that was so different.

"I delivered my message and they said they'd come. They didn't. Not for several hours. By the time they did, it was nightfall and your mother was beyond help. She died just before morning. Your father couldn't bear it. The blame. He couldn't take it on his shoulders. So he found it convenient to tell everyone the fairy tale that she died when she had you. Half of it was true. She wouldn't have died if she didn't have a baby. But neither would she have died if he'd brought the doctor home on time.

"He chose Felicity over his wife. And he conveniently blamed you, CeCe."

"Why didn't you ever tell me, Uncle Alex?"

"Your father was raising you as he wanted, CeCe. As long as you were under his jurisdiction, we all went along with the lie. Even Aunt Susan Elizabeth. I determined I would tell you someday when you grew up. I was waiting for the right moment. Here and now"—he gave me an apologetic grin—"with me cutting open a hooded merganser, up to my elbows in blood and my knees in mud, isn't my idea of an ideal time to tell you."

"What is?" I asked.

"Ah, you're going to give me mouth. Well, I deserve it."

"No, Uncle, I'm sorry. You don't."

He shrugged. "I should have told you sooner. He did

you a serious disservice, your father, putting all that guilt on you, saying you had no soul, telling you you were the thorn in his side. It's unbelievable how we can create our own legends and make them true." He shook his head. "Or others can create them for us."

Then something occurred to him. "Will my telling you the truth erase all your guilt, CeCe?"

"I don't know. I'll have to study on it."

"You do that, sweetheart."

He'd never called me "sweetheart" before. The endearment warmed me.

"Lord, I need a bath. Look, we'll talk more about this when I feel more human. I promise. Now would you get ahold of that man Sammy and ask him to ready a bath in my room? I've still got to visit with the sick servants yet. And interview Old Tom. You want to come with me to the slave quarters?"

"Yes, sir. I do."

About seven o'clock in the evening the slaves began to gather in the planter's yard and light bonfires to clear the air. Then they would start to sing their slave songs, softly at first, and in rhythm with the night breezes.

Uncle and I and Earline stood and listened at first, then we went on down to the slave quarters.

"You too tired, CeCe?" Uncle asked. "You've had a long day."

"No, sir, though I've been awake since they blew that bugle at four o'clock this morning."

"Ah, the conch shell. It's to wake the slaves. That's the time they get up. Doesn't seem fair, does it?"

"No, sir."

He smiled. "Still think slavery is nothing to be concerned about? Wait until you see the sick ones."

"Do they have anything she can catch?" Earline asked.

"If they do, I'll handle it. Thank you for your concern, Earline," Uncle said.

We went to the slave cabins. They were crude things. One-room places, made from logs. They had dirt floors and they smelled.

Inside were a couple of beds, a bench, a table, and two cooking utensils, a griddle iron and a great big pot on a rack. I thought of the big house. I thought of Uncle Alex's kitchen with its shining copper pots hanging from the racks. I thought of his study, his library, his studio at home.

Horace the turkey had a better place to roost than this.

The beds were corded with rope. There were six people in the cabin. I wondered how many had to sleep on the dirt floor. They all looked up as we came in.

There were three children seated on the floor next to the chimney, which was made out of sticks and mud. Two were crying. Two women were pregnant, far along and lying on the corded beds. Another, who looked as if she had the mumps, was leaning over them. Around her head she had a small sack tied.

"Have a headache, do you?" Uncle asked her. "Does the jimsonweed help?"

"Yassir," she answered.

Uncle turned to me. "CeCe, have you had the mumps?"

"Yes, sir."

"All right. Then you can stay."

He set his doctor's bag down and opened it, apparently accustomed to a place like this, not at all taken aback, willing to do the best he could.

Earline was taking notes as fast as she could.

"What have you had for the mumps?" he asked the woman with the jimsonweed tied around her head.

"Fresh marrow from the hog's jowl will cure 'em," she told him. "Had it this mornin'. No need to worry."

Uncle reached into his bag and gave her some kind of powder. She took it. He then directed her away from the pregnant ladies. Then he leaned over them and spoke softly. One cried out in pain when he touched her.

"CeCe, go outside," he directed. "Earline, come. I need help."

I stepped out into the dark, obediently. From inside I heard his voice, talking soothingly to the pregnant woman, heard her wail, heard him saying "two weeks."

"Allst I need is some sulfur in my pocket," I heard her saying. "I won't hardly pick up no sickness if'n I got sulfur on me."

"All you need is to keep clean. I'll send up to the house for some clean sheets and quilts for you to lie on. I'll tell your mistress it's necessary or she'll lose a good worker," he said. "And now I want to tell you ladies something else. All right, CeCe, you can come in now."

I went in and heard him tell the three women about the way north, the safe houses, the way to cross a stream as quickly as they could so the dogs would lose their scent, the North Star, and how the two pregnant women should not leave until their babies were at least four months old. That would bring them to November. It was cold in the North in November.

But there would be no snow yet in Ohio. The people in the safe houses would keep them if there were.

He gave them money.

I wanted to cry, watching my uncle in the lamplight, being all doctor and all abolitionist at the same time.

His birds were forgotten.

His birds were all around him.

He was teaching them to fly.

My heart filled with love for him. I wanted to run over and hug him. Why should he care about these people? He had everything he needed in life and more.

And then he cautioned them not to tell that he'd shown them the way to run away. Or he'd either be shot or hanged or tarred and feathered.

And "Oh Lordy," one of the pregnant women said, "why would we do this to the Lord's own angel like you?"

The one woman who wasn't pregnant said she wanted to pray. And so he prayed with them. They prayed *for him.* What kind of God, I wondered, would not take care of him?

We left shortly after that. There was nothing much to say, walking back in the dark.

We had to have dinner yet. He had to sit down at table with the owner of the slaves and act like he believed what the man believed in.

"Damn," Mr. Abraham said, "I've got at least six prime nigras down with some sickness or other and we've been giving them all a dose of garlic and whiskey every day to keep them well. Even the children."

I knew Uncle Alex well enough by now to see that he was trying to hold in his anger. He hunched his broad shoulders forward. That was a sure indication. "Cleanliness is the answer," he said mildly. "And keeping those with the mumps away from the others."

"These people wouldn't know what cleanliness was," Mr. Abraham said. "Damned children are as thick as blackbirds around here. Can't keep 'em away from one another. We'd like to see some of your drawings if you have time tonight. Wouldn't we, dear?" he said to his wife.

"Oh, I'd love to."

"You shall," Uncle agreed. "After I interview Old Tom." He cleared his throat. Another sign that he was desperately trying to control his anger.

Earline had to go down to the mulatto quarters and eat, so I fetched the box of drawings for Uncle. And after he interviewed Old Tom, he laid them out on the Persian carpet in the front parlor.

They exclaimed over the beauty of them. "The brushstrokes do not pretend to be anything but what they are," Mrs. Abraham said, "and yet they render the birds more alive than they are in life."

She begged for some drawings to put in the museum in Savannah, but Uncle had to say no, they were to go in a book. He had so many subscribers already, in America and England, who had given money.

Before we left Greenbriar they gave him money to be

subscribers for his book, too. "We are true patrons of beauty and the creatures God made," Mrs. Abraham said.

I thought that if God heard her He might strike her dead, considering the condition of their slaves. I opened my mouth to say something, but Uncle's look stopped me.

Mr. Abraham hired us a coach. And he just happened to know of a driver who came with it, a "decent sort of fellow looking for work. You'll like him. He knows the roads, the countryside, the plantations. He'll also be an excellent guide."

I can't honestly say that I've ever been positively influenced by a fat man, but I never saw Ralph Parsons as fat. I just saw him as Ralph, the minute I met him. He was immaculately attired as a coachman, convinced Uncle that he could handle horses, had a pleasant face, knew when to keep his tongue still and when to speak up.

He respected Uncle. He respected me. And more than that, he respected Earline, which, I told myself, was something to watch. From the minute they met he knew she was nobody's slave, though he didn't give away her secret.

Uncle kissed Mrs. Abraham's hand and we got into

the coach, and I would not let myself think of the little negro babies to be born in the filth of the cabins in the quarters.

We left, with shouts of the Abrahams' blessings trailing after us, to find our next plantation.

Chapter Eleven

THE ABRAHAMS sent us off with baskets of sweetmeats and fresh fruit and gave us the name of a friend with a plantation on the other side of Savannah, on the other side of the dark woods that seemed to stretch into eternity. But Ralph advised us not to go to the plantation, that he'd heard of slave unrest there. Anyway, he'd heard that the scarlet ibis had been sighted on the rice plantation of a lawyer-merchant-planter named David Richards, nearer to the ocean.

We took a southeasterly course and soon were in those woods, where Earline started to tell the stories of Indians. Especially when we passed a place called Murder Creek.

It was in a deep glen and there was a burnt-out tree stump, very large, in the middle of it.

"This is where the Indians attacked," Earline said dramatically, "fifteen years ago. About twenty whites had been camping out overnight and the Indians leaped on them and killed them all."

I moved a little closer to Uncle on the seat.

"All right, Earline, that's enough. These woods are frightening enough for a child. Don't you have any nice stories to tell?" he asked.

"I know one," Ralph said through the isinglass window. "There are said to be elves in these woods that come out at night. There's a tollhouse up ahead, and if you're good enough to go to heaven, the elves will let you through without paying. Of course you can't see them in daytime. But they can see us."

Sure enough, we came upon the tollhouse, the first building we had seen, and inside the little box was a man who looked like an elf. Ralph stopped and talked to him and he waved us on without making us pay.

We went over the wooden bridge across a river. Uncle smiled.

"Thank you, Ralph."

My mouth was open. I was just about to say he was lying, that I wasn't seven years old anymore and far past fairy tales, when I saw Uncle smile.

"Ralph knows all the tales, doesn't he, CeCe? And of course, the tollbooth man would never charge us on what is still Mr. Abraham's property. But it's not far past reality, that story." He winked at me.

As we went on, the woods got thicker and Uncle pointed out the little dark avenues that led off the road, one after another, it seemed. Where did they go?

"They look like paths made by lumbermen," Earline commented.

"They are roads leading to plantations, every one of them," Ralph told us.

Then he started to slow down. "Accident, sir," he called from up front. "You want me to stop?"

"Of course," Uncle said.

Earline and I craned our necks. We could see an overturned stage up ahead. On the ground were sprawled three people. Ralph stopped and Uncle, cautioning us to stay inside, reached for his doctor's bag, and he and Ralph got down to see what they could do, if anything.

Earline and I almost upset the stage peering out. "Do you need me?" she called out to Uncle.

He waved her out. The woman was moving and Earline jumped down and went right to her and I remained, jealous that I was left behind, to my own imaginings.

It turned out that the driver was dead, that the man and woman had been lying there all night, near a stream, that they were battered and terrified. All the man had was a pistol to shoot any snakes or wolves or attackers.

Uncle called to me then to bring the three blankets we had with us. Gladly I responded. And I stood there watching while he attended to their wounds. The woman's arm was broken, her face and forehead were cut. The man's leg was broken. Uncle made splints out of nearby wood, and after he had used all the bandages in his doctor's bag, asked Earline to take off her petticoat, which she did immediately saying, "Yes, master," going into her act without a second thought.

He used it for bandages. He ripped it up and gave me the pieces to soak in the stream. I was so glad to be part of it all, I forgot to be frightened. I brought the wet, wrung-out bandages back to him. He wrapped the woman's forehead.

"My head is throbbing, Doctor," she told him.

"Get my flask," he ordered me.

I fetched it from the carriage. It wasn't until I watched him give her a powder and hold the flask of liquor up to her lips that it came to me how painful all this must be for him, how it must jog his memory.

An overturned stage. One dead. One broken leg, an injured woman.

But he went about his business as if the other accident had never happened.

Then he and Ralph wrapped the man and the woman, who were husband and wife, in blankets and put them inside our stage. There was plenty of room.

He put Earline on the floor.

Ralph examined the wallet of the dead driver and announced that he worked on the plantation where the young couple came from.

"We must wrap him up and take him home," Uncle said. And so they proceeded to wrap the broken body and put it on top with the couple's luggage.

Their name was Englebert, the young woman told us. "We're just coming back from our wedding trip. Tipton came to Savannah to pick us up. Oh Lord, what will Papa say that he's dead?"

"Papa," it turned out, was one of the richest planters in the area.

"Our plantation is White Hall. You all will be welcome to stay. Papa will be most grateful to you," she went on. Her name was Jorja, and we offered her some fruit and sweetmeats. She was starving.

Her husband, Albert, had passed out.

It was a grim ride we took that afternoon through the dark woods. Especially now that I knew that the thumping overhead was not only luggage but a dead body. Uncle fell asleep, huddled against the quilted side of the carriage, and Earline dozed on the floor. Jorja was soon asleep, too, and so it was as if I were the only one alive in the world as we bumped along in the shadows.

And then, by four o'clock, and I know it was four because I stole a look at Uncle's pocket watch, we came out of the woods and to a wide creek where there was a small village.

"South Newport River, sir," Ralph called down.

I shook Uncle's arm, and he awoke and ran his hand over his face. "What is it? Another accident?"

Our guests were still asleep. "No, sir," Ralph told him. "We've reached the settlement at South Newport River. It's a stopover in the woods, a short way yet to the avenue where the young people live, but I thought you might want to get out and stretch your legs, get some refreshment, and take stock of things."

"Good idea, Ralph," Uncle said. "Come on, CeCe, Earline, let's get out. Sunlight! After all that dark. It's worth the price alone."

The day's heat was abating. The river was full of sloops and barges that were bringing ashore different kinds of goods that were being sold on the spot by merchants. Colorful tents filled the shoreline. There were weeping willows and ducks in the water close to the shore and some sailor was playing a mouth organ.

"Uncle, I smell coffee," I said.

"It's French coffee." It was Jorja. She'd gotten out of

the carriage to follow us. "You'll love it. I frequently stopped here with my father."

"Where is your husband?" Uncle asked, reaching out a hand to her.

"Still passed out in the carriage. Or sleeping, I don't know which. I want to bring him some coffee."

We stayed a while at the settlement, where we ate some twisted and salted pastries and drank French coffee. We found privies. Uncle revived Jorja's husband, Albert, and then we got on our way again to continue in the dark, thick woods until we came to the right avenue that led to White Hall and Jorja's home.

It was four miles down the dark road, between overlapping rows of trees, Jorja told us. It was getting on to dusk now and in the distance we could see the lights of the plantation house.

In the woods to the side, at one point, I thought I saw the forms of people, dark forms slithering about.

"Uncle, I see people," I said. "Look. Are they hunting?"

"No," Albert said, "they're runaways. Damned runaways. Hundreds of them live in these woods. Come back to the plantation at night to steal. If I had the old man's permission I'd shoot 'em dead. But he won't give it, no. Says they'll starve soon enough. Says how long can they live on berries? Berries?"

He looked at us. "Ha. They break into the corncrib, the meat house at night. They're not living on berries. They get figs and oranges in the fields."

"Albert, don't get excited," Jorja said. "It isn't good for you in your present condition."

Albert sank back in the chair. "Got to pull myself together," he said, brushing off his coat arms and his pants. "Got to answer to your father for this accident."

"You don't have to answer to anybody, does he, Dr. McGill?" She started to brush him off, too. "If you were my father, would you call him to account?"

"No. It wasn't your fault, you weren't driving." Uncle Alex cleared his throat and I could tell he was thinking of another accident, the time he was driving.

I was surprised to see the ocean in the far distance. But not that far, it seemed. For the house was built on stout poles, at least five feet off the ground, in case the ocean decided to go beyond its boundaries and come in, Uncle said. Underneath the large stucco house grew some vegetation, and there were goats nibbling at it and dogs lying in the coolness of the structure. The house was surrounded by pine trees, oaks, twisted cedars, and palmettos.

A small, furry, three-legged dog came to greet us, yapping his gladness. He leaped up to Jorja's shoulder and she held him. I loved dogs. At home Uncle had two, but they were hunting dogs and not to be spoiled with petting and fondling. I missed my own.

As soon as our carriage drew up to the house some honey-colored servants came to help us out. They fetched down the body of Tipton, and the luggage.

Jorja's mother and father came down the steps, and when Jorja saw them she cried all over again as she blurted out her story. Her father, Mr. Ardley, listened solemnly, held her close, and almost smothered the three-legged dog between them. Then he went to examine the body of Tipton and give orders to have him taken away.

Jorja's mother was near tears, but as a true Southern lady introduced herself as Caroline and insisted on introductions all around. We were then taken inside and "accommodated." Dinner was almost ready. It was near eight o'clock. We were shown to our rooms.

Mine overlooked the faraway ocean in front. It turned out that I could hear the steady swishing of the waves, like a clock in my ears all night long.

In this house Earline was to sleep on a mattress on the floor at the foot of my bed. There were no lustful brothers. The only other male in the house was another visiting doctor. His name was Hepplewhite. And we met him at supper. He was older than Uncle and his area of expertise was fever. He had studied in Ireland, he said. "In Meath Hospital. Under Dr. Robert Graves."

"Didn't he believe in building up fever patients' resistance?" Uncle asked him.

"Yes. They starved them in Dublin and I built up their resistance. I'm trying to analyze what brings fever on."

If I pretty much ignored their talk, I could imagine I was in a dream. Candlelight sparkled off the delicate chinaware on the lace tablecloth. Small negro girls fanned the room to keep it cool. Notes from a pianoforte drifted in from a far room. Mr. and Mrs. Ardley were dressed in formal wear, as was Uncle Alex. I was told by him to wear one of my new dresses he'd had made in Savannah. Earline, now in the kitchen, had done my hair and put a string of pearls in it.

We ate cold roast beef and turkey, ham, pâtés of shrimp and crab, punch, syllabub, fresh fish from the ocean, and biscuits so light they might fly away, with butter in the shape of butterflies, more of that French coffee, and a special cake for the bride and groom. Not to mention sherry, which Uncle said was the best he ever had.

Afterward we went to the solarium, which was all glassed in and filled with plants, and from where a mulatto servant was playing the pianoforte. We drank more coffee with thick cream. Uncle said if I had any more I wouldn't sleep. But I had more anyway.

I was sent to bed by Uncle at ten. I slept, despite the coffee. The sound of the ocean put me to sleep. Earline promised to wake me at eight for breakfast, though I was certain I wouldn't be able to stand the thought of more food.

At eight the next morning I was up and dressed in my velvet riding outfit to go riding with Uncle and Jorja, who despite her broken arm insisted on riding anyway. Albert was not yet fit for such an exercise.

The horses were sleek and lively, yet manageable. Jorja showed us the cattle her father raised, the sheep, the horses, as well as the cotton that was planted after the rice was harvested. It was a successful plantation, Uncle Alex said.

I thought it was paradise. But that afternoon, when Uncle Alex went off riding on his own and I was left to my own pleasures, I found out that it was hell.

Chapter Twelve

UNCLE ALEX was going to ride down that long road we'd come in on, he told me.

"Into the woods. Where we saw the slaves. I don't want you with me. They may attack. I don't want you hurt."

"What about you?"

"I know how to talk to them. Don't worry. Just find something to do. Go out on the beach. I hear there are shells. Or go into the library. I won't be long." He kissed me. I hated to see him ride off. He took his gun and some painting supplies in case he saw "any goodly birds."

I asked Mrs. Ardley if I could wander down to the beach. She said yes. She offered to send a servant with me. Earline, she had discovered, could read tarot cards. "I must have her read mine this morning. And then she is going to do my hair. I did so like the way she did yours last evening."

I said no to the servant. "Thank you, ma'am, but I can go alone."

She gave me a pail for collecting shells. I left her and Earline there at a small table in the back parlor. The sun was not out. The clouds were closing in. An atmosphere of possible storm loomed on the horizon. As I went out of the house and past some fencing, I saw in the distance a small cemetery and perceived that some negroes were digging a grave for Tipton. His funeral was to be held tonight.

The negroes had their own small church on the place. So small it looked like a child's playhouse. Yet it had a steeple and a cross on top. I walked on the path past the cemetery on my left, past the kitchen gardens on my right, and through the tall sea grasses into the sand.

Yes, there were shells. I could see them up ahead. Jorja had said to watch for the sand-colored curly ones. But what was that I'd just seen out of the corner of my eye?

Someone else digging a hole? Why, it was Dr. Hepplewhite. I hadn't seen him at breakfast. And here he was digging a hole in the sand.

Next to him was a negro boy about fourteen years of age, wearing only a long shirt that reached below his knees. I hid behind the tall sea grasses so I wouldn't be seen. What was the good doctor doing?

The hole looked to be about three feet deep and three feet long, if I am any good at my arithmetic, which I am not. Two and a half feet wide.

Soon Hepplewhite stopped digging and threw what looked like dried red oak bark into it. Quantities of it. Then he lit it and made himself a respectable fire. It burned and burned, and then he put a plank across the bottom of the pit. And then a small stool.

My mind raced. Fever. He was studying what makes fever. I felt bile in my throat and for a minute I thought I would throw up my breakfast of fish and waffles and hominy and coffee. I could taste it all.

In the next moment, sure enough, he made the negro boy take off his shirt. Now he was naked.

I had never seen a naked boy before. Uncle Alex would have a kitten if he knew I was looking at one now. But I didn't care about his nakedness. It didn't interest me. What held my interest was what I knew was going to happen next. And it did.

Hepplewhite—and I knew I could never call him Doctor again—ordered the boy into the pit. The boy sat on the stool with only his head poking out of the ground.

Then Hepplewhite took out a thermometer and tested the heat in the pit.

Satisfied, he gave the boy something to drink. Then wet blankets were laid across the hole and over the boy's head, and stones were laid down to keep them in place.

It wasn't long before I saw the mound of the boy's head slump over. He had fainted.

Hepplewhite pulled back the blanket and lifted him out and laid him on the ground. He felt his forehead and wrote a few notes down in a notebook. Only then did he revive the boy.

"You have a good fever," he said to the boy, who moaned and rolled his eyes so that just the whites of them could be seen.

I forgot my shells. I forgot the ocean. I left the pail so I wouldn't make any noise and I crawled in the sand so I wouldn't be seen. I couldn't be seen, I thought. Not even by God. Because if He couldn't see that poor boy, how could He see me? And then how could Hepplewhite see me?

Having decided thusly, I stood up and ran as fast as I could.

"Hey there! Who's there? Who is that? Stop!"

I froze. I turned and faced him.

"You sneaky little girl. You're the niece. Do you spy on your uncle's experiments, too?"

I shook my head no.

"Then how dare you spy on mine? Don't you know

that a doctor's experiment is sacred? We experiment like this all the time in Europe. How do you think we make headway with disease?"

I didn't much care at the moment, but I knew better than to say.

"You're a rude and impudent little piece, and I've half a mind to tell your uncle and have you punished."

"Please don't, sir," I begged. At once I slipped into the role I knew I must play for Uncle Alex's sake. I knew I must not, at any cost, give away that my uncle was an abolitionist or that any of this had appalled me.

While on the plantations we must behave as if we believe as they do. Uncle had schooled me. Hepplewhite laughed. "He'll spank you good, if I tell him you were spying on me."

I knew better, but again I didn't say anything.

He waved me away disgustedly. "Brat. Get out of my sight. Why do I bother?" He turned to the boy who was moaning.

I ran. In the distance the sky rumbled with thunder. It was even darker than before. I was usually afraid of thunderstorms, but now I didn't even consider such a fear. I had seen hell this morning on this beautiful plantation.

My breath was spent when I got back to the house. The three-legged dog leaped at me, and I picked him up and held him against my shoulder. Why did he only have three legs? Nobody had said. I brought him into the house and put him down and he ran for Jorja, who was reading to Albert in the library.

She looked up. "Are you all right?"

"Yes. Is my uncle back yet?"

"It's not yet been an hour. Why don't you wait for him on the porch? Or under the porch? I used to wait for Papa to come home there as a child. Take Henry with you."

"Henry?"

"The dog."

"Oh yes. Come on, Henry. I think it's going to rain, Jorja." My voice cracked. I wanted, so badly, to tell somebody about Hepplewhite and what he was doing to that poor boy, but something warned me that if I told Jorja now she would say, "Oh, yes, he's doing experiments" and go right on reading to Albert.

Henry came with me, and we went out the front door and down the steps and underneath the house. We sat there under the porch, Henry in my arms, waiting for Uncle Alex. Henry was the only one who could appreciate what my mood was, I think. He was shivering.

Chapter Thirteen

"UNCLE."

He lay on the bed in his room, bootless, in his trousers and shirt.

"Not now, sweetheart. Earline, fetch me a bit of that sherry. They do have excellent sherry here at White Hall, along with their food and accommodations, if their practices with slavery do make sick the soul."

"This is hell, Uncle."

"I don't like that kind of talk from you, CeCe, though I can understand your lack of adjectives for what you've seen. I've heard all about it from Dr. Hepplewhite. And about you. I've promised him I'm going to punish you severely. Do you prefer the cat-o'-nine-tails or the slave driver's whip?"

"Uncle, don't joke."

"It's called desperation, CeCe." He was propped up against ruffled pillows. His face was scratched. Earline was applying cooling cloths. "All right, Earline, that's sufficient, thank you."

"I tried to tell you when you rode in, but you said 'not now' to me then, too."

"I'm sorry. I needed some time to myself. And then Hepplewhite grabbed me. We've both got to apologize to him later."

"Apologize?" I almost choked on the word. "He's the devil."

"Sometimes one must make deals with the devil, child. You may go, Earline."

She smiled. "If you don't need me anymore, sir, Mrs. Ardley wants another reading of tarot cards."

"Are you keeping in your role?" he asked.

"Yes, sir. I call her ma'am. I curtsy. I stop to fetch her tea. I do everything I'm supposed to do."

"Good girl. Go then, don't keep her waiting, and for heaven's sake just give her good readings."

He turned to me. "I want to thank you for not giving vent to your feelings with Hepplewhite, for remembering what I told you about honoring their practices. You may have saved my life this morning, CeCe."

"The boy fainted, Uncle. Only then did he let him out of the hole."

More silence on his part. "I'm sorry you had to stumble across this, CeCe. He should have had sense enough to do his god-awful experiments in a far corner of the plantation and not in full view of anyone."

"You're worried because I saw a naked boy, aren't you?"

"I'm not exactly elated."

"I wasn't interested because he was naked, Uncle. I was afraid for him. I wanted to grab his hand and run away from there."

"I respect your feelings, CeCe."

"What are you going to do about it?"

"I told you. To keep our image we have to apologize to him for your spying."

"I can't do it, Uncle."

"I'll apologize for you. I'm responsible for you. But as far as doing anything, there's nothing I can do, child."

"Nothing? Look what you did this morning. Helping all those runaways. You did help them, didn't you?"

"Yes, thank you for asking. I gave at least half a dozen directions north. In secret. You know the difference. I can't help this boy because a doctor does not question or interfere with another's experiments. And because I'd be asked why I care so much for the little slave boy. The boy is Mr. Ardley's property. I cannot disapprove or I'll be suspected of being an abolitionist."

I was trapped. "You have to agree with everything they believe in," I said dully.

"Exactly."

"So one boy continues to suffer. And maybe die."

"Yes."

"But you ride into the woods to save six others."

"And how many more after that, CeCe?"

"One doesn't count?"

"You have answered your own question, CeCe. You are starting to understand slavery."

"Well, I don't like it."

He gave a small smile.

"You knew this would happen to me," I accused him. "That's why you brought me along with you. You couldn't leave me be. You had to drag me through the mire that killed my father and might yet kill you. Well, I'm not there yet. And I might never be. I want you to know that."

He nodded and said nothing.

I felt tears in my throat. I wanted to lash out at him. I wanted to hurt him. And then I thought of all the good things he'd done for me, how kind he'd been. Was he like a spider, luring me into his web? Is that what this was all about? I sniffed and wiped a tear from my face.

"I don't like this place anymore," I told him.

"Are you sure you're not saying that you don't like me anymore?"

"I want to leave here," I said stubbornly.

"We'll take our leave tomorrow," he promised. "Now bring over that light blanket and make my excuses for lunch. I want to nap."

I fetched the blanket and flung it out over him. He reached for my hand and held it. "It's all part of growing up, CeCe," he explained. "Growing up is never easy. I'm just here to help you along the way. You have a right to be disappointed in me. Any time you decide you don't like my help anymore you can go back to Aunt Susan Elizabeth. I think it would be foolishment on your part, but I promised you that and I keep my promises."

I nodded my head and left the room.

HE WAS ALONE in the front parlor having a before-dinner drink, all gussied up, his mustache waxed and his long black hair combed back.

Uncle took me by the hand and brought me into the room.

"Ah, Dr. McGill, have you yet sighted the scarlet ibis?"

"I thought I did this morning, but it got away."

"Would you like a drink?"

"No, thank you. I want to apologize for my niece's actions this morning. They were unforgivable and I've punished her severely."

"As you should." Hepplewhite looked at me, waiting. Uncle squeezed my hand. I knew what he wanted. "I'm sorry for spying on you, Dr. Hepplewhite," I said.

He nodded his head in satisfaction.

"You may go now, CeCe," Uncle said in a most formal manner. "I'll see you at dinner."

Hepplewhite was smiling in satisfaction. I wanted to throw a vase of flowers at him.

Chapter Fourteen

WE LEFT THE next morning and traveled for a whole day. Like Mrs. Abraham had done, Mrs. Ardley gave us a basket of food—cold chicken, warm bread, oranges, cake, milk for me and Earline, and a bottle of sherry for Uncle. She even gave a special basket for our driver, Ralph.

I felt both grateful and frightened to be leaving. Of all of them I would miss Henry the most. And I would be haunted by the negro boy. Would he undergo more experiments? Would they kill him, finally?

Uncle gave Ralph directions. He wanted to visit a rice plantation on one of the nearby islands. He had a feeling there would be birds on the islands that weren't on the mainland.

We traveled for two hours, all the while looking out

the windows for birds in the trees we passed. And for one minute I took my eyes off the tree branches and looked on the ground.

"Uncle, a bird."

"Where?"

"On the ground. We just passed it. Tell Ralph to stop."

He did. We both got out and walked back to where I'd seen the bird. It lay on the ground, on its back, feet up, dead.

Uncle squatted down. "It's a snowy owl. He's accidental in this state."

"He's got brown spots."

"Yes. Where's Earline?"

"She's in the carriage talking with Ralph, showing him her notebook."

"Getting rather friendly, aren't they?"

I said nothing. I knew when to keep my own counsel, especially when it concerned Earline. But back at the Ardleys' I'd seen them out walking together. Twice.

"I suppose they've been thrown together, her being always put with the servants," he said. "Well, I must go and fetch my canvas bag. Don't touch him now, honey."

He went. The bag was large and cumbersome and held his bird equipment. Inside he found his measuring tape and notebook. "Twenty-two and a half inches," he said. "And look, the bill is almost hidden in the feathers." He took out a linen cloth and wrapped him in it.

"His wing is broken. He couldn't fly. He must have just starved to death here. A fine specimen. You did well, CeCe. I shall sketch him and send a watercolor to my friend John Francillon in London. Come, let's get back in the carriage."

Carefully he put the bird in the canvas bag.

We resumed our trip, with Uncle making more notes about exactly where the bird had been found and how it frequented the lower parts of the country. Sitting right next to him, I could read his writing. He was so happy about the bird, he suggested we open our basket and have lunch here and now without stopping.

After lunch Earline and I both slept until he woke us. We'd come to a river and a huge ferryboat would take us across to what was known as Newfield's Retreat.

Ralph knew of it. "The woman's a widow," Ralph told him. "Lost her husband four months ago and lives here with her baby son and her fourteen-year-old brother. She's lonely, word has it, and loves company. Looks forward to it, Doctor. I'm sure she'd be honored to have you."

"It's one of the reasons I hired you to squire us about, Ralph," Uncle said. "You're a regular guide of lower Georgia."

The river was wide but becalmed. From our position on the ferry we could see what looked like half a dozen negroes on the wharf on the other side. They were waving and singing at our approach. When we finally arrived, they seized the ropes that the captain threw and tied the boat up. And when our stage rumbled off they surrounded it and jumped up and down looking in the windows until Uncle, afraid that we'd run them over, ordered Ralph to stop.

"You all best clear off or you'll be hurt," he told them.

"Who come, who come?" they clamored.

"Tell your mistress it's Dr. Alex McGill from Ohio, and he's a sketcher of birds."

They ran up the hill. "They'll never get it right," Uncle told us. "Likely they'll tell her it's Mr. Ohio from McGill and he's a doctor of birds. But it's all the same thing, isn't it?"

The house was the usual white-columned affair, draped over with trees. I was accustomed to such houses by now. This one sat on a hill overlooking the river, like Uncle's house did at home. But somehow it twisted my innards when I saw it. For I sensed it was different. And I was right.

As it turned out, it was the only plantation we visited that Uncle did not meet with any slaves and encourage them to run off.

"OH, COME IN, come in, I am so glad you are here!"

The woman's slaves, the ones who had greeted us at the wharf, took our things, brought us cool drinks, and loitered around and stared at us, anticipating our every move.

They sat at our feet in the handsomely appointed parlor and listened. I should have known something was amiss by the way they never left her.

As if taking her cue, Earline sat at her feet, also.

Her name was Mrs. Ditmas. She appeared young in her yellow calico, and it was obvious that the slaves adored her. But she also appeared uncertain of herself, even frightened.

"Where is Robert?" she asked no one in particular. And as if in the wings, waiting to be summoned, a handsome young man came into the parlor holding the hand of a smiling little boy of about three.

"Michael." She held out her arms. "Come to Mama."

The boy ran to her. She scooped him up, kissed him, and set him down. "This is my only child," she introduced him. "And this is my brother, Robert. He lives with me."

Uncle nodded and shook hands with young Robert, who glanced over the heads of the slaves at his sister with a look I could not interpret but obviously she could. She clapped her hands and said, "Out, out, we'll see you all later."

And the slaves scrambled out, like a flock of birds. Uncle gave a look and Earline went with them.

I could see Ralph smoking a cheroot outside the long windows. When Earline made her exit to go outside he was waiting for her and they went off together.

How long, I wondered, had this been happening? How long had Uncle and I been blind to it? It posed no problem, except that Ralph was white and Earline was negro.

"Up North, perhaps," Uncle's voice behind me said quietly, "in Boston or Philadelphia, this would be accepted. Down here he could be hanged. She could be whipped. I must talk to them both."

"I am never free of them," Mrs. Ditmas said of the slaves who had just left. "They come and watch me write letters. They watch me sew. They trail after me when I visit the meat house and the buttery. I feel as if I have a tail."

"Is there a reason for this?" Uncle asked.

"Yes. Primus is trying to kill me."

"Who is Primus?"

"Under my husband, he was our best worker. The other field hands all looked up to him. He obeyed my husband, but since Jeff died, he is impossible to control. He weighs about two hundred and twenty pounds and Jim, our overseer, quit because he cannot keep him in line. Primus has committed great outrages. He steals from other plantation owners. He has beaten one owner to within an inch of his life. He drinks. He undermines my abilities to control my other field hands. Yet I am responsible for him.

"I'm afraid he's going to kill someone. Or me," she said again. "He's threatened my brother here, with a knife."

"Don't you have any other man to turn to?" Uncle asked. "Another relative?"

"No. It's what happens on so many plantations when the husband is away for an extended period of time or he dies," she explained. "The woman ends up being afraid for her life."

"So what will you do?" Uncle asked.

"Sleep with a pistol next to me. Oh yes, I know how to use one. And sell Primus. I have Mr. Isham Gordon, the Georgia slave trader, coming in two days. Primus must be sold out of state to a vigilant master. Don't you agree?"

I could see the thought wheels in Uncle's head turning. Would he take it upon himself to convince Primus to run away?

"Will you all stay until Mr. Gordon comes?" she asked him.

"It isn't going to be an all-out slave sale, is it?" Uncle asked. "My niece has never seen one. I'm afraid it isn't the kind of thing I'd want her to see."

She nodded understanding. "Only Primus," she promised. "I need all the others to run the place. Desperately."

I heard a bell in the distance. "Dinner," she said.

Uncle took her arm. A negro nurse took the child. I was left with Robert, who stood looking at me.

"What did you do when Primus threatened you with a knife?" I asked him. He was taller than I. A man already at fourteen. His sister would soon have herself someone to run the plantation.

"I ran," he said. "But now I carry a pistol. I soon learned to use one."

"Who taught you?"

"You mustn't tell."

"Of course not."

"Munro. One of the negro servants."

I gasped. "He knows how to use a gun?"

"Yes. And it was a good thing. He protected me from Primus. He was the only protection we had until I learned to use my Colt here." He patted his hip. It was hidden under his frock coat.

"So your sister knows, then. So who mustn't I tell?"

"Anyone else. Or they'll go crazy and take Munro away. The whole idea of it, a negro with a gun. Come," and he held out his arm to escort me into dinner.

I went with him. The whole dinner was as civilized and as tranquil and sumptuous as on any other plantation we'd been on. They did it up well anyway, dining. Never mind what went on outside the dining rooms in these places.

Chapter Fifteen

"I ASKED ROBERT to ride out with me tomorrow and look for some birds. He declined." Uncle shook his head. "I thought you two were getting friendly."

He was having sherry, alone, on the front piazza. I had gone in to say good night.

"He has to protect his sister," I said.

"I saw he wears a pistol. Can he use it? Foolish question. All Southern boys of fourteen can ride and shoot. Why didn't he shoot Primus when he attacked him, I wonder."

"He hadn't yet learned to shoot then. But he knows how now."

"Ah, yes."

"Uncle, are you going to tell Primus about the North Star?"

"No. Why unleash such troublesome habits and a vicious nature upon the North? He either belongs in jail or an insane asylum."

"Is there anyone else here you're going to tell the story to?"

"No. Our hostess is alone in the world. She needs all the help she has to stay solvent."

Silence on both our parts. From somewhere we heard a bird call. "The common nighthawk," he said. "Maybe I'll find one tomorrow. You coming with me? Or do you choose to keep Mrs. Ditmas company?"

"I want to come with you."

All talk of slaves, of his leaving them to help Mrs. Ditmas who "needed all the help she could get to stay solvent," was forgotten.

I had often wondered if there was a line he would not cross in talking slaves into leaving. If he would ever see the slave owner's point of view.

Now he spoke, as if he could read my mind. "I'm not coming down on the side of slavery, CeCe. I'm coming down on the side of a woman who's alone in the world and trying to keep hearth and home together. I'd like, if the situation were the same, for someone to do likewise for my wife. If I saw cruelty around here toward the slaves, I wouldn't keep my tongue. I haven't seen any."

"Yes, sir."

"Don't 'yes, sir' me. Tell me you understand. And you're not disappointed in me again."

How could I convince him? We were still conducting ourselves under the cloud of our last disagreement.

I simply went over to him and put my arm around his shoulder. "I understand, Uncle," I said.

He put down his glass of sherry. Of a sudden the cloud over us disappeared. He took me on his lap, something he'd never done, and held me for a moment. "Am I forgiven, then, for my inactions with Hepplewhite?"

"Yes, sir," I said.

He kissed my forehead. "Thank you. Now go to bed. Breakfast is early. We're off at eight tomorrow."

IT TURNED OUT that the slaves on the Ditmas plantation knew all about the Ever-After Bird. And when they found out who Uncle was, and that he was riding out to look for it, the house slaves crowded around us the next morning giving us gifts of song and flowers, biscuits wrapped in towels, sweetmeats likely stolen from the kitchen.

"Bring the bird, bring the bird," they chanted. "Bring the Ever-After Bird."

We rode off, I, Uncle, and a reluctant and pouting Earline. Ralph held her horse for her, helped her on. I minded, she who was so independent and self-sufficient now needed help mounting her horse. Of a sudden she had become meek and coy and retiring.

Ralph had wanted to go with us. "I can help Earline so she doesn't have to labor so," he proposed.

"It's her job and she doesn't labor so," Uncle said testily. "She has to complete her duties so she can honestly record them and write about them. You and I will talk about it later this day, Ralph. Anyway, Mrs. Ditmas can use a man around, besides her young brother. And you know how to use a gun. Keep watch over her."

That day, as we rode through grasslands, rice lands, woods, and swamps, Uncle found and shot two birds, the wood duck and the great egret.

We had dismounted our horses near a rice field when we sighted the egret.

Uncle showed me through his binoculars. "He's so white," I said. "And tall." *And beautiful,* I told myself. *Please don't shoot him,* but I knew better than to say. If I did voice such opinions, I'd never be allowed out on trips with him anymore. Something of the child in him there still was that hurt every time he brought down one of these lovely creatures, so I kept silent.

We watched the egret for a while. "He frequents the rice ponds around Savannah," Uncle told me. He readied his gun. "Now look away, CeCe, if it bothers you."

I turned away. The shot echoed across the water of the rice field, announcing in a hollow, drowning voice the end of something. But Uncle knew how to shoot it without destroying its beauty. He held back Earline, who made as if to fetch it, and sloshed out in the water himself. I didn't see the shot bird. He put it in a canvas bag.

The next, the wood duck, we watched for a while in its habitat. Uncle pointed out how they built holes in the cypress trees along the edges of the swamps, high from the ground.

"The mother duck carries the young one to the ground in her bill," he told us, "and if the young one is captured and put in a pail or a tub, it can climb out with the aid of its bill or claws."

"The duck is colorful, Uncle," I told him. "You'll need a lot of watercolors."

"Yes," he agreed.

Then we went through the business with the shooting again. "It's the male," he told us, "not the female. So if she's got little ones up there, they won't be motherless."

Another explosive sound of that shot. I shall never get used to it. It reverberates in my heart. How can a gentle, honorable man like my uncle Alex, a man who fixes people who are broken, do this? Have I yet to find out?

THE NEXT DAY, the slave trader, Mr. Isham Gordon of Savannah, Georgia, came riding up the long drive in his wagon, with a negro assistant carrying a whip and a long gun.

Primus was lying on his bed in his quarters, three sheets to the wind, thanks to the efforts of Robert and Munro. Robert, with his mother's approval, had given Munro enough liquor last night for both Munro and Primus to stay in their cups until Christmas.

Munro stopped drinking short of midnight. He was sober enough to lead Mr. Gordon and his assistant to the quarters of Primus, who was taken in hand, tied and bound, and led out into the sunshine to be examined by Gordon.

Mrs. Ditmas seemed relieved. "He's in prime condition," she told Gordon. "Not a mark on him."

We stood, the lot of us, in the barnyard watching: Mrs. Ditmas, Robert, Uncle, Munro, Earline, Ralph, and myself.

"CeCe, go into the house," Uncle said.

But I did not move. I watched Mr. Gordon open Primus's mouth and examine his teeth. I had seen Uncle do this with horses. I watched him run his hands over Primus's naked back and shoulders. I had seen Uncle do this with my own Pelican.

"Give you one thousand," Gordon said.

"He's worth twelve," Mrs. Ditmas countered.

"My father paid eleven," Robert put in.

"All right, twelve," Gordon said. "If I can buy the girl, too."

"What girl?" Mrs. Ditmas asked. "I'm selling no girl."

"That one."

And he gestured toward Earline.

I heard a gasp and realized it came from me. I covered my mouth with my hand. Earline gave a nervous little giggle. Ralph moved a little closer to her. Uncle spoke.

"She's mine. I own her. I'm on an expedition. We're from the North, and I'm not selling."

Mr. Gordon smiled. "Fine specimen like her. Prime breeder. I could get fifteen for her down in Mississippi."

Earline went a little crazy then. I think the word "breeder" caused it. She lunged at Mr. Gordon and Lord knows what might have transpired if Uncle hadn't reached out, grabbed her arm, and stopped her. Then he shook her good and slapped her face.

Earline cried out. I gasped again.

"Go into the house!" Uncle ordered sharply. "Now! CeCe, take her in. Move!"

But it didn't end there. Ralph stepped forward when Uncle slapped her, as if to attack Uncle, who grabbed him by the shoulders and whispered something to him. God knows what, but all the wind went out of Ralph and he was the one to walk a crying Earline into the house.

"You go along, too, CeCe," Uncle directed.

Robert came along, too, upstairs with me. But instead of going into the room I shared with Earline, he halted in the hallway and drew me close to him.

"Is he that strict with you?" he asked.

His eyes looked into mine. "No," I said. "Now I have to see to Earline."

"Ralph can see to her. Haven't you noticed how smitten he is with her?"

"Yes."

"Trouble there. Your uncle will have plenty to deal with. CeCe, I'd like to kiss you. May I?"

"If anybody sees us . . ."

"I don't see anybody, do you?" And with that he put a hand on either side of my face and drew me toward him, and it was sweet and tender and I felt as if I'd been waiting all my life for this moment.

When we were finished, he smoothed back my hair. "C'mon," he said. "I'll take you inside to see Earline."

She was lying on her bed, a cloth on her head. Ralph was standing over her.

"He had no right to hit me," she told me.

"No," I agreed. "But if you attacked Gordon, you'd have to be whipped. He'd have to let the man whip you. Uncle knows that." I took the cloth and wrung it out in the water basin and turned to apply it to her face again. "Even I know such things by now."

"He hurt me."

"Of course," I said. And I was thankful he wasn't like my father, the kind of man who would take it in his head to hit me. So there is another side to him, I thought. Is it the side that kills birds? Or is it the side that survives? And do we all have it, without knowing it?

Oh, I had so much to sort out, so much to think about.

Uncle Alex came into the room, examined Earline's face, and apologized.

"I had to," he said.

"I know," she told him. "CeCe explained it to me. How they would have had me whipped if I attacked him."

He gave me and Robert a look, took the cloth from Ralph's hands, dipped it in cold water, and applied it again to her face.

"I told you to take care of her, CeCe," Uncle said. "What have you been doing?"

"I've been with Robert. Talking."

"When I needed you?" He was angry and chose to ignore Robert. "Is that how I can count on you?"

"Sir," Robert said, "it's my fault, I—"

"CeCe can speak for herself. She knows what I expect from her. She's got herself to blame, if anybody. Now why don't you two men go about your business and let CeCe stay with Earline until she falls asleep. Come on. Ralph, the carriage needs to be packed. Robert, doesn't your sister need you for something?

"But first get me my doctor's bag, CeCe. I want to give you a powder so you can rest, Earline. We're leaving this afternoon."

I fetched the bag and he gave her the remedy. I stayed with Earline until she slept. Then I packed both our belongings, Earline's and mine. We had a cold repast out on the back piazza, and for once the household slaves didn't sit around Mrs. Ditmas as we ate.

She was cheerful, grateful, almost girlish. "Now I can hire an overseer," she told Uncle Alex.

Ralph readied the carriage and horses, packed our belongings, and with a basket of Mrs. Ditmas's favorite foods we readied to take our leave.

I WAS SAYING good-bye to Robert under the cypress tree on the side of the house. There was a sadness in saying good-bye.

I had given him my address in Ripley, so he could write to me. This would not be the end of our friendship.

"My sister says I may come North to college," he told me. "And if I do, I'll come and see you."

"Yes," I said. "That would be wonderful."

"Would your uncle allow it?"

"I'm sure he would."

"Is he very strict with you?"

"No, he just pretends to be. He's a dear."

"I saw him slap Earline. My sister never hits our slaves."

"He had to or she would have attacked Mr. Gordon. Then she would have been whipped. He did it to save her from herself. He's never hit her before."

He nodded, understanding, and held my hand. "I wish I were leaving now," he told me. "I'm starting to hate this place." He said it fervently, with all the passion of a young man who wanted to ride off and have an adventure. "I wish I could kiss you again," he said.

Of a sudden I wished he could, too. Should I let him? For a moment I wavered, and then I thought, *If I got caught, if he got caught,* and it was lucky I hesitated, for in the next instant I heard my name.

"CeCe."

Uncle came around the house. I could see him through the leaves of the cypress tree. "Yes, Uncle."

He came forward, saw Robert holding my hand, and said, "We're ready to leave, come along."

"Yes, sir."

Robert brought me around to the front on the brick walk, still holding my hand. I could have let go, but didn't. It was sort of a promise to him. There was no other way to make one at the moment.

Again Uncle saw this, but said nothing, as he loaded the canvas bag with his birds.

"May I kiss her on the cheek, sir?" Robert asked Uncle.

"I think a kiss on the hand would be proper," Uncle Alex answered.

Not to be thought improper, Robert bowed and kissed my hand. The sun shone on top of his head and I wanted to touch his hair, but I didn't dare. *He looks like a knight,* I told myself. *When I write to him, I shall tell him so.*

When I got into the carriage and looked out the window, I saw tears gathering in the corner of his eyes as he stood next to his sister, waving. The house servants were all gathered around singing some song about flying away. That didn't help me any or help those tears in Robert's eyes. I waved until we were well down the drive and out of sight.

"Robert's going to write to me," I told Uncle as we settled ourselves inside.

"Well, at least you can't hold hands over a thousand

miles of country," he said sardonically. But he didn't scold. "Anyway, I have other things to worry about."

And he glanced toward Earline, who was gazing up through the isinglass window and talking to Ralph. What he intended to do about this, I could not imagine. But he did intend to do something.

Chapter Sixteen

"EARLINE," Uncle said, "close the window."

She closed it.

"We have to talk, you and I," he said. "I'm sorry it has to be in front of CeCe, but it can't wait. Earline, you know I respect you as a person and I admire your work at Oberlin and I'm going to write a good report about you, but I'm afraid you're about to throw it all away and I can't let you do that."

He glanced at me. "CeCe, read your book."

I had picked up one of the romances we'd bought in Savannah, but it was paling in comparison to this. I pretended to read. The third Earl of Devonshire had just decided to disguise himself as a beggar and roam the streets of London to find the woman he loved, who'd been banished from the palace of her father, the King, for loving him.

"You can't stop me, Doctor," Earline was saying. "I love him."

"Do you realize what you're *about,* child? Even being *seen* with him here in this part of the country could earn both of you terrible consequences."

She lowered her head. "'Love is not love that alters when it alteration finds,'" she said softly.

"Don't quote Shakespeare to me," he said sternly. "We're talking about death here. For him certainly. For you, maiming."

"Then let's go North," she said. "Now. Ralph will come with us."

"I'm not finished with my work here. Neither are you. We need to visit at least two more plantations before we leave."

"I hate the South," she said petulantly.

"So do I, Earline. But for my work, it's a virtual paradise, a treasure trove of discovery. My mistake was placing you in a position of being a slave. You've been maligned and insulted and demeaned."

"I wanted it," she admitted. "I want to write about it for my work. And it isn't that you're objecting to. It's Ralph. But I'm telling you again, Doctor, that I love him."

"Negro and white courtships aren't acceptable anywhere, Earline. Except maybe Boston or Philadelphia. Now I'm responsible for you on this trip."

She said nothing for a moment. Then, "What do you want from me?"

"I want you to be discreet. As discreet as possible. No outward shows of affection. No secret meetings. After we get home, you are your own person, but while you're here, you are as accountable to me as is CeCe. Are we agreed on this?"

She lowered her head. "Yes, sir," she said. But she raised her eyes just enough to look at me, and in those eyes I saw defiance as clearly as I had seen those tears in Robert's eyes.

"UNCLE, CAN WE stop the carriage?" I asked desperately a while after this discussion.

He sighed. He was near to falling asleep. "Can't you wait, CeCe?"

"I'm going to wet my pants."

"You could have gone back at the plantation, but no, you were too busy doing other things before we left. All right." He sat up, leaned forward, and rapped the isinglass window over Earline's head. "Ralph, we have to stop."

"Righto, sir."

We were on a lone road. Where we were going, I didn't know, and I don't know if Uncle knew, either, but he trusted that Ralph did.

"Earline, want to get out and go with her?" he asked. "I don't want her being alone."

We jumped out of the carriage. All around us were woods, deep Georgia woods, and tall grasses, the sound of birds, the shadows of animals scurrying about, and trees draping down their branches.

Earline and I looked at each other. "Up a little bit, away from the carriage," I said. "In case Uncle gets out."

We walked on the side of the road, about a hundred yards from the carriage. It was then that she told me.

"I'm going to wed Ralph."

"Well, Uncle said you could be your own person when we get back North."

"I mean here. In the South. As soon as I can."

I stopped walking. A furry creature scurried across the road in front of us. "How?" I asked. "And when?"

"I don't know. The first how and when I get. These plantations all have church services."

"But they won't marry negroes to whites. You heard what Uncle said."

"They have ministers who might. They have negro reverends. They have their own secret services. I found that out, eating and sleeping with the slaves."

I'd forgotten about that, what she must have learned living with the slaves in their own surroundings. The secrecy she must have learned. How to fool the white people.

She was no longer our Earline. She belonged to two worlds.

"I'll do it first chance I get," she told me again. "And if you tell your uncle, I'll tell him you kissed Robert."

I stopped walking. "I never kissed Robert," I lied.

"He won't know that. He won't know who to believe now, will he?"

We found a place. Earline gave me my privacy while I passed my water.

How was I to keep her secret from Uncle? Was I to keep it from him or tell him? Why had she told me? Did she secretly want me to tell him?

It was then that I smelled the smoke. And heard the faint sound of bells. And I forgot my other troubles.

Quickly I finished my business, pulled up my pantalets, adjusted my skirts, and told Earline. We looked around and soon found the source of the smoke.

A negro man, or creature resembling a man, was bent over a fire made of sticks on the side of the road, roasting sweet potatoes.

It was a man, sure enough. But on his head he wore a strange circle of iron that fastened under his chin and around his neck. A second circle of iron fit around the crown of his head. The two were held together with three rods of iron. They looked like horns and stuck out at least three feet above his head and on the end of the rods were bells.

"My god," Earline whispered. "I've heard talk of such a contraption, but I've never seen it."

"What is it?" I asked.

"It's what a master uses to keep a slave from running away, after he's whipped him and it doesn't work. The man's likely been told he can wander wherever he pleases, because he can't go far wearing that. He wears it day and night and it probably weighs about fifteen pounds."

"How can he sleep?"

"He can't. Come, we must talk to him."

"I'm afraid."

"What kind of a ninny are you? This man's been through hell. He's in it now." She commenced to walk toward him and I followed.

"Hello," she called out.

The man looked up. His shirt was in rags. So were his britches. He was without shoes. His face bore scratches from the underbrush. "'Lo, missee, you from the carriage that jus' passed?"

"Yes. My name is Earline. This is my little charge

here, CeCe. My master is in the carriage. Do you need help?"

"I'se a runaway, chile. But I cain't go far. Thas' why my massa put this thing on my head. So everybody would know I'se a runaway. I been a-wanderin' in these woods fer three days now. Grubbin' sweet potatoes and cookin' 'em over the fire. An' lookin' fer the Ever-After Bird. If'n I sees him I knows I gonna be free somehow. Did y'all see him?"

"I know about the Ever-After Bird." I stepped forward. "My uncle, in the carriage, is seeking him." And in as few words as possible I told him about Uncle Alex and his work.

His face brightened. "Would he come back to the plantation wif me? If'n he would, my massa would forgive me fer runnin' away. If I could bring back so 'portant a man as him, I'd be forgiven sure 'nuf." He nodded his head. The bells rang.

For a moment I was convinced that the whole world had a streak of madness in it. I said yes, Uncle would come. I ran back to the carriage.

There I opened the door and blurted out my story to Uncle about smoke and how I thought the woods were on fire and a man with fifteen pounds of iron on his head and bells that rang was cooking sweet potatoes over a fire and the man was wanting us to come back to his plantation because he was a runaway.

"CeCe, do you have a fever?" Uncle fairly lifted me into the carriage, and felt my face. "Has the climate in this low country finally caught up with you? Or did you fall and hit your head, child?"

"No, sir, it's all really happened. Earline is back there talking with him."

"And she's let you wander off alone? Do I have to talk to her again?"

"No, sir, Uncle, you have to come back and see the man. Please?"

He said yes, he would come and see him.

IT TURNED OUT Ralph knew about the plantation up ahead, and it turned out Uncle had wanted to visit another coastal plantation because he had intelligence that the Ever-After Bird was seen in these parts. So he accepted, if warily, the invitation of Angus.

Angus refused to get into the carriage. In all fairness, he wouldn't fit with that absurd headgear of his. He loped ahead of us, the bells ringing on his head, while Earline scribbled furiously in her notebook and Uncle leaned out the carriage window and peered ahead.

We passed more thick woods, more low, reedy

swamps where the cane rattled in the breeze like soldiers' swords.

And then I heard Uncle say, "My god, another one."

He meant the plantation, I discovered, when the carriage crunched along the stone drive and the house came into view.

This white mansion was more luxurious than all the others, with steps going up to the columned piazza, groves of orange trees, sunken gardens, hedges of oleander and boxwood.

They grew cotton, not rice. "Somehow the rice culture, with its wet, unhealthy work, makes them all crazy," Uncle said as the carriage came to a halt. "Let's hope cotton makes them fare better."

The master and mistress of BelleVille, as it was known, were on the drive to meet us, surrounded by a number of slaves. And as we got out, there was Angus, kneeling on the stones, hands clasped in front of him.

"Welcome to BelleVille, I'm Mr. Gainor," the man said to us.

The first thing he figured Uncle might like was a cooling julep, but Uncle corrected him, saying no, the first thing he wanted was amnesty for Angus, who was kneeling on the stones of the driveway so still that the bells on his iron headpiece were silent.

"Ran off again, did you, Angus?" Mr. Gainor cheerfully asked. He was embarrassed about his slave, about the headpiece, about the fact that Angus had brought us to him, about everything.

"This man know 'bout birds, massa," Angus offered humbly. "'Bout the Ever-After Bird. I brung him to you, you forgive old Angus."

"A deal is it?" Mr. Gainor looked at Uncle. "They're always making deals. I know the headpiece looks dreadful, but it's the only way I can keep him on the place. Now you all come in out of the heat. The sand flies are especially thick today. Charlotte, instruct their servants where to go. And the little girl looks like she needs refreshing. Have Tessa show her to her room."

I was taken upstairs by Tessa, a slave, and helped with my washing and changing. My new calico frock from Savannah was suitable, she assured me. She even brushed my hair.

"There's rattlesnakes about an' they get themselves up into the trees," was the first thing she told me.

Then, "He a doctor-man, your uncle? I heared he be."

I nodded. How had she heard so soon?

"He best be careful and mind hisself then. The slaves hereabouts gonna be all over him wif their complaints. You tell him not to believe half he's gonna be told. My, you got pretty hair. Where be your mama and daddy?"

I told her.

"So you a orphan child. We got plenty o' them on this here plantation. Your uncle be your daddy now, is that it?"

I said yes, in a way.

"There be only one way," she said. "He either be or he not be. You lucky to have him. You be good to him. Men always need us women to be good to them. They act real brave, but they sometimes be more scared than us. 'Times we women need to be the real brave ones. You may never have run into such times yet, but you will. There, your hair real pretty now. Make your uncle-daddy proud when you go downstairs to have good eatments."

She couldn't have been much older than Earline. Why couldn't Earline be as nice to me as she? Because Earline was free and she was not? Was I preferring the friendship of a slave here to a free negro woman?

I thanked her and she seemed surprised at being thanked. She brought me downstairs into the solarium, a room adorned with plants and gilt cages filled with birds, where Uncle was walking about, inspecting them, naming them, and saying things like:

"The black skimmer. This one looks to be about seventeen inches in length. Always to be met with on the sea coast and islands. What will you do with him?"

"I intend to set him free in a while."

I wished he could say the same about Angus, who was still running around with that set of iron antlers on his head.

We headed in for dinner, which again was a cordial affair.

Afterward, when the harsh sun was setting and the day began to cool, we sat on the back piazza. Mr. Gainor sat there with a pistol lying in his lap. "In case a rattlesnake appears on the steps," he told Uncle.

I was tired but wouldn't succumb to it. I listened to the adult talk, which consisted of the price of cotton in Savannah and Mr. Gainor bragging about his married daughter who was in Europe. Then a man slave came and stood just below the steps.

"Time, massa?" he asked.

"All right, Leo," Mr. Gainor said. Then to us, "He's going to let loose the watchdogs. I always do at night. They won't let anything come 'round this place," he said. "If, for any reason, you have to fetch your servant in the quarters, just go into the kitchen and get some sausage. They'll be your friends instantly. Like most of mankind, they have their price."

"Good thing to know," Uncle said.

We heard the sound of an iron gate, the rush of the dogs, their sniffing and running, then silence, until I heard something else.

The low, unmistakable sound of singing.

"The servants are having a prayer meeting," Mr. Gainor told us. "Now some plantation owners don't allow their slaves to gather for devotions, but I do. I find that religious meetings are innocent enough and even make them more trustworthy."

"And the singing is beautiful," his wife put in.

"Uncle, can I go and see the service?" I asked.

"No, CeCe. It's private. Anyway, you heard about the dogs. And I'm not about to go into the kitchen and get any sausage unless it's for a good purpose."

"Do you think Earline's there?"

"Most likely."

It came to me then. Earline had said that on some plantations the negroes had their own services. And when she found such a service she would get married to Ralph.

She was likely getting married this very minute, while we sat here sipping coffee and looking at the stars and talking about the price of cotton in Savannah and the innocence of the slaves' devotionals. And I hadn't even told Uncle she intended to do so.

Chapter Seventeen

I DIDN'T SAY anything to him that night because I didn't know for certain if she had done it or not. Maybe she'd only been tormenting me with her talk of marriage, trying to make me look like a fool if I ran to Uncle.

Anyway, before I went off to bed, when Mr. and Mrs. Gainor went to see about tomorrow's doings on the plantation, the slaves appeared, like ghosts in the night, looking for Uncle.

"Suh? You be a doctor?"

"Yes."

"You come, please? We got sick chilluns."

He went for his doctor's bag and his pistol, and when I tagged along and asked to go with him to the cabins, he said no at first.

"But you may need help, and Earline is nowhere about," I argued.

He looked at me sternly, my "daddy-uncle," then his face softened and he said all right, but I was to stay close to him.

We went to the kitchen for the sausage, found some, then a lantern, and the waiting slaves gestured we should follow them into the night.

"A great many young ones have died this year," one of the elder slaves told Uncle. The slave was well spoken. "The Lord has mercifully removed them from this life of misery and shame."

Some dogs came over, sniffing, growling. Uncle handed out bits of sausage and they let us pass. We came upon the cabins, more to be described as huts. There were children everywhere, it seemed, running about half naked.

"Take the well ones outside," Uncle instructed one of the slaves. Then he nodded hello to the mothers and out of his pocket took some chips of sugar, which he'd likely also gotten from the kitchen, and gave it to the sick children as he examined them, one by one.

It quieted their crying. "They don't have fever," he told one mother after another. There were three of them. "They just have colds and congestion." Out of his bag he withdrew a bottle and gave it to them. "Before they go to bed, give them each a spoon of this."

They looked at him questioningly.

"Spoon," he said. "Spoon."

"Oh." One mother picked up a large wooden one from the mantel of the fireplace.

"No," Uncle said, "that's too big. Give them half of that. Half. Do you understand?"

They nodded yes. And he turned to the fourth baby being held by the mother. He held out his arms and she refused to give it over. Now he reached into his doctor's bag again and withdrew a necklace made of seashells and offered it to her.

I gasped. Where had he gotten it? How had he known he would need it?

She took it greedily and handed over the child. Uncle set the child down and examined it briefly, shook his head, and took the blanket it was wrapped in and rewrapped it, covering its face. "This child is dead," he told her.

A chill gripped me. The mother gave out a screeching wail and raised her hands to the heavens. "I always lose them," she cried out. "This is the third one I have lost."

"You must bury it tomorrow," Uncle told her. "I am sorry." Then he turned around and looked at the others. "You need better clothing for the children," he said, "and for yourselves. You need to fetch more fresh water to wash with. And you need soap. I shall tell your master."

They fell upon him then, thanking him. He was barely able to pick up his doctor's bag, his lantern, the canvas bag of sausage, and grab me by the arm and make it outside.

There we stood in the starlit night. Uncle took my hand.

We walked for a while and then he stopped. I thought he saw a snake. But all he said was, "That woman killed her baby."

"Sir?" I asked.

"She smothered him. There was no sign of illness. She smothered him to keep him from living in the misery and degradation that he would face if he lived. And likely she killed the two she lost before him, CeCe."

I said nothing.

"Come," he said, "and keep your eyes out for rattlesnakes."

I held his hand tightly. This, I decided, was likely one of those minutes Tessa had told me about, when he needed me to be good to him, when he was acting brave but he was more scared than I.

"YOU'D RATHER have Tessa dress you than me," Earline accused when Tessa left my room to get a curling iron.

"I didn't say that. I only hoped to relieve you of some of your chores. Anyway, you're supposed to be Uncle's servant, not mine."

It was the next morning. She'd come to my room to help me dress. But I was finished already, garbed in my riding habit, and Tessa had only to do my hair. Earline was late and I knew why.

But I waited for her to tell me.

"Curling iron," she scoffed. "You're going out riding, looking for that silly bird, and she's going to curl your hair in stupid round curls. Why don't you wear braids like you do at home?"

"Uncle likes the curls."

"Ten minutes in this humid weather and your hair will be straight as a reed."

We were walking on eggs here, talking about everything but what we wanted. Finally she said it.

"Last night I wed my charioteer."

I just stared at her. "You didn't."

She nodded firmly. "At the prayer meeting. They had a visiting reverend. We married. He bedded me last night."

"Did you tell Uncle?"

"No. No reason for him to know."

"No *reason*? You could get killed for this down here

and you say there's no reason? He's the one who has to protect you. He has the right to know."

"Then you tell him, little miss Goody Two-shoes."

"You're scared, so you want me to do your dirty work for you."

She took a deep breath. "Why should I be scared? He'll scold, even though he has no right. Anyway, I've a husband now to protect me."

No, I thought, she has no reason to be scared. I do. Because I should have told him last night. And I didn't. I was going to catch hell for what she'd done because I hadn't warned him. And she knew it.

Tessa came back with the curling iron and made long round curls. I went down to breakfast looking like a princess. Uncle scowled at me because I forgot to say good morning to our host and hostess, and then I just sat and looked at my food and didn't eat.

"Are you ailing?" he asked.

"No, sir."

"If you don't eat, you don't ride."

I ate. Conversation was pleasant. I even laughed once when Mr. Gainor told how he'd gone to Savannah to purchase a parrot for Charlotte, and the bird had joined in the conversation about the price for himself, saying, "Too high, too high."

The parrot was to be delivered next week. We wouldn't be here. Uncle was going to attempt to talk to some slaves today about the route north. I knew that Angus was on his list. I also knew that he was deeply concerned about that thing Angus wore on his head and how he could travel with it. And if it were at all possible to get it off. He'd told me last night.

I felt surrounded by life-threatening happenings, between Earline's wedding and Uncle's doings. I ate my fish and eggs. I left only a tiny portion of grits on my plate. Uncle didn't scold.

Out on the trail in the pinewoods, I told him about Earline's wedding. In what must have been the loveliest corner of creation, it was the unloveliest conversation we'd ever had.

"She *what*?"

He brought his horse to a halt. And so I brought mine. "Married, sir."

"When? And how?"

"Last evening. At the prayer meeting."

"Did you know about this?"

I wanted to lie. Oh god, I wanted to lie. Instead, I dived right into those ice-blue eyes and drowned myself. "Yes, sir."

"Since when?"

"A couple of days now."

"Why didn't you tell me?"

"I thought she was only teasing me. Making a joke. And if I told you, I'd make a fool of myself. She does things like that to me all the time. But last night when we heard the music, I knew it, sir. Nobody told me, but I knew it was happening."

Nothing now but those ice-blue eyes staring at me. And the sound of a bird flying over. The Ever-After Bird? If it were, I daren't break the silence. *He's going to do something terrible to me,* I thought.

"What in God's name am I going to do about this?" he said. Not to me. To the trees, to the birds, the rattlesnakes, maybe. Not me. He'd rather talk to the rattlesnakes at this moment.

"I don't know, sir," I said.

"I thought I had your trust, CeCe."

Oh, there it was, the worst. What I'd been dreading. "Uncle, I'd rather you beat me than say that." There was a controlled sob in my voice.

"Yes, well, I told you once I only do beatings on Thursdays. This isn't Thursday, is it? Well?"

He was playing with me now. Did that mean he forgave me? "No, sir, it's Wednesday."

"Then you'll have to wait until tomorrow." He nudged his horse forward and I followed. We rode abreast. "What she's done isn't your fault and I shouldn't blame you. But I do blame you for not telling me. You understand?"

"Yes, sir."

"Very soon you and I are going to have to talk. About trust. And another matter. Especially since Earline has gone and done this fool thing. Boys. Anybody ever talk to you about boys?"

"No, sir."

"The way you carried on with Robert."

"I didn't carry on."

"Well, you were too free with him. We're going to have to talk about all that. Now I've got to concentrate on Earline and Ralph and how I can keep them from getting killed down here. This way, let's go this way. I see some slaves over there in a corner of the cornfield. Is that Angus?"

It was. He was attempting to hoe some corn. In the middle of the field were some skinny little children, waving their arms, looking like scarecrows, scaring the birds away. We dismounted our horses and Uncle went over and stood under a tree. There was no overseer.

Soon several slaves were gathered around him, including Angus. He started talking about the Ever-After Bird, asking them if they'd seen it. If asked about this meeting later, he could always blame it on the bird.

Then he commenced telling them about the North

Star and the way to get to Ohio from here. I walked a distance away. I could not abide the look on Angus's face. He was so still that the bells did not even ring on his headpiece, and when the other slaves had received their money and their instructions from Uncle and gone back to work, he remained.

"How I gonna travel in this thing?" he demanded.

"I've brought something that might help, but if it does, you'll have to hide out the rest of the day and leave tonight," Uncle told him.

He nodded. He was ready to do anything. Fear gripped me.

"CeCe, lead the horses away from here. Meet me by those pines on that hillock."

I started away. Like Lot's wife in the Bible, I looked back once to see Angus seated under a cypress tree and Uncle trying to get the headgear off with some sort of knifelike apparatus he had.

He fussed with it for a good ten minutes. Then gave up. I saw him hand Angus the same money he'd given the others, and shake his hand.

"I couldn't get it off," he confessed sadly as he walked up to me.

We went on, riding into the pinewoods to look for the Ever-After Bird.

We did not find it that morning. Uncle's heart wasn't

in the search. "I'm worried about Earline," he told me. "I've got to talk to her, caution her about things. We'd better ride back."

In the barnyard we handed over our horses and he told me to go and change for our midday meal. Seeing that he was in a mellow state of mind, I lingered while he inspected the other horses.

"Uncle," I said.

"Yes, CeCe."

"I've been thinking."

"Always a bad thing to do, child. What is it?"

"If you could just hear me out without scolding."

"I'll try."

"Maybe she just loves him so much she can't help it. I mean, doesn't that count for something?"

He'd been patting the nose of a brown mare. He went on patting, not looking at me. "It counts for all the world, CeCe. There isn't anything else that counts as much."

"Well then?"

"Do you remember Hepplewhite? And the boy? Did that make sense to you?"

"No, sir."

"These people down here are different. What counts to them makes no sense to us. It's that simple. As nice as they are, inside they're all Hepplewhites. I'm trying to save her from them. Now if you don't understand that, CeCe, I might as well send you back to Aunt Susan Elizabeth, because I've made no progress with you."

"I understand, Uncle."

"Good girl, now go change. They're having a guest for lunch. I saw a fancy carriage in the front drive. Go make yourself pretty. We must keep up our part of the charade."

"RAININ' AN' the sun be out," Tessa said to me as she put a towel around my shoulders to do my hair. "That mean the devil be whippin' his wife behind the door."

Again we went through the business with the curling iron. Earline came in, looking quite downcast and different from before, and I assumed Uncle must have already spoken to her.

"Did you hear the news?" she asked.

"No," we both said.

"They found Angus. Drowned. In the deep part of the stream. About an hour ago."

Tessa almost dropped the curling iron. My mouth fell open. My hand flew to my breast. "It can't be," I said. "When we went riding, Uncle and I, we saw him hoeing in the cornfield this morning with the other negroes. He waved at us as we rode by."

"Maybe he got tired of hoeing," she said.

"Angus can swim," Tessa protested.

"And he could also drown himself if he wanted to, with that thing on his head," Earline reminded her.

Tessa compressed her lips and continued curling my hair.

"They found money in his pocket," Earline went on. "Mr. Gainor figured he stole it and was afraid he'd be caught and whipped and so he killed himself."

She looked straight at me when she said this. I breathed a sigh of relief. At least they wouldn't be pointing fingers at Uncle.

"We'll have to bury him tonight," Tessa said. "He was always trying to run away. Suppose he was tired of trying. He couldn't go far with that thing on his head. You'd best get down to the dining room, CeCe. Your uncle-daddy won't want you to be late. I've got to go and help plan Angus's funeral."

She left us. Earline sat down on the bed and said nothing for a minute. Then she spoke. "That uncle-daddy of yours can surely put the fear of hell into a person when he chooses to," she told me.

I nodded yes.

"I'm not to look at Ralph with any special meaning. I'm not to walk near him. I'm not to hold his hand or be caught in the same cabin in the quarters with him. Or Ralph might be dead. And I could be whipped. Do I want to be whipped again? he asked. What did he want me to say?"

I kept a still tongue in my head.

"I pray God I can do this until we get home. One more plantation after this, he says. One more." She sighed, stood up, and smoothed her skirt down. Tears were in her eyes. "I'm going to fetch his drawings. He's going to show them in the parlor after lunch."

Chapter Eighteen

"DO YOU ALL think a small fire would be amiss?" Mr. Gainor asked his guests. "With that rain before, I think we've had a bit of cooling."

Everyone agreed that a small fire would be delightful. Mr. Gainor called in Marshall, one of his house boys, to make one. Then he said he hoped the rain hadn't ruined the cotton that hadn't yet been picked.

The guest was a Mr. Pope, a tall, thin man from Augusta, who owned a large cotton manufactory there. The conversation at lunch was all about his travels around the country with his "Georgia plain cloth."

"I'm trying to get the planters to buy it for their negro clothing," he explained to us, "instead of buying Northern cloth. It would relieve them of the tariff on the cloth they are buying from up in the Northern states."

"Makes sense," Uncle said, "though I come from the North."

Mr. Pope glared at him as though he were personally responsible for the tariff.

Then they spoke of other things Southerners were buying from the North and paying tariffs on, and there was a great deal of bitterness in Mr. Pope's voice. Mr. Gainor gave him an order for his cloth then and there, and the man brightened considerably.

To my surprise, Earline helped serve the dinner. Her head was turbaned and she was very decorous, and I saw Mr. Pope giving her some admiring looks. Uncle saw it, too. And he introduced the subject of the Ever-After Bird and how we'd spent the morning looking for it.

This turned the attention, for some reason, to me.

"How old is your niece?" Mr. Pope asked.

My age was given by Uncle.

"Down here she'd be in our year-round girls' academy near Macon, Georgia. Or the Montpelier Episcopal Female Institute. Under the direction of the Right Reverend Stephen Elliott, Jr. The school offers a full corps of competent teachers for all branches of English education."

"I intend, after she finishes the village school in Ripley, Ohio, to send her to Oberlin College," Uncle said firmly.

Mr. Pope scowled. "I've heard of Oberlin. Teaches women to be upstart troublemakers."

"She's an upstart troublemaker now," Uncle quipped.

Everybody laughed but Earline. I thought she would drop her bowl of hot fresh beans right on Mr. Pope's head. Fortunately, Charlotte said something about her own schooling in London, England, just then and everybody laughed some more, lightening the mood. Then a negro from the barnyard came in and announced to Mr. Gainor that Militia, one of his mares, had dropped a mare foal within the last hour and it was "very healthy and a bay color."

"Very good, Horace," Mr. Gainor told him. And then I giggled, and Uncle scowled at me. The rest of them looked at me peculiarly and Uncle had to explain about Horace the turkey at home and it made for another story.

Outside the rain had started again. Inside the fire crackled. The soup was excellent. The drumfish was tasty, the red potatoes cooked to perfection, and the beans Earline almost dropped as tender as could be.

And nobody mentioned Angus, who at that moment was being wrapped in a winding-sheet in the quarters, I supposed, as they readied him for burial, the iron headpiece still on his head. Would Mr. Gainor have it removed for burial, I wondered?

I had to ask Uncle.

———

He did remove it, because that night, when under the negroes' torchlight we all attended the funeral, there was no headpiece on Angus. He was buried in the negro cemetery and they sang their spirituals and all the white men in attendance, including Mr. Pope, had their pistols at the ready in case of rattlesnakes.

Earline stood with the negroes on one side of the grave and Ralph with the whites, on the other. She never even glanced his way. And then, at the last moment, when the coffin was lowered into the ground by two strong negro slaves, it happened.

A terrible thing happened.

A rattlesnake slithered into the grave and landed on top of the coffin.

It was Uncle who first had his pistol out, and he shot it without injuring the coffin. The shot rang out. The negroes never missed a beat with their song. But something inside me stopped for a moment and I thought, *What kind of a mad place is this, where a man is dead because he wore a piece of iron that weighed fifteen pounds on his head? And at his funeral a snake coils itself on his coffin?*

I walked close to Uncle as we left the cemetery.

"Are you all right?" he asked.

"No, sir," I answered. "Uncle, I want to go home."

He put his free arm around me. In the other he held his lantern. "Yes, I know. This is not a nice world we've ventured into. I want to go home, too. I miss my wife dearly."

"Do we have to visit one more plantation?"

"It's been said the Ever-After Bird is in these parts. There's a plantation just down the road apiece. It's said to be a nice place."

"They're all nice places," I said bitterly.

He squeezed my shoulder. "You're learning, CeCe," he said tenderly, "you're learning. Be patient with your old uncle now. One more place after this. I'm with you. That's all you need to know."

"DOWN THE road apiece" turned out to be some twenty-five miles as the Ever-After Bird would fly. It took us a whole day to get there. Earline was writing furiously in her notebook. And drawing, despite the bouncing of the carriage. I found out on this trip that she could draw quite respectably.

When she was finished she showed us a likeness of Angus with the headpiece on his head.

As an artist himself, Uncle said it was very good.

There were other drawings, too, but she wouldn't let us see them. Uncle said we must respect her privacy and wait until she wanted to show them to us. He understood her need for secrecy, he told me.

We arrived at the next plantation near sunset. It turned out that Mr. Gainor had sent a rider ahead to tell them we were coming and they were ready to receive us.

Here the house was plain, no sunken gardens. There were the usual oak, cypress, and long-leaved pine trees, yes. There was a profusion of dogwood and laurel and magnolia, all uncontained and sprawling and near covering the landscape.

The house was more like ours at home. Mine, I must remember to call it now. The farm where I grew up. White fencing, horses grazing, ceiling-to-floor windows on the house itself, dormers at the top. It struck some chord of familiarity inside me that such houses would always strike.

And I discovered something more about myself. You can cherish the memory of a certain place even though what happened to you there was not always happy.

The owners were Mr. and Mrs. Nourse.

Mr. Nourse had whiskers that stuck out on the side of his face, and I didn't like him on sight. Mrs. Nourse was long faced and submissive, and in five minutes I determined that she couldn't come up with an opinion of her own if her life depended on it.

The slaves skirted around him, obeying his every command almost before he gave it.

His overseer, Bench, was white, and one of the first things Mr. Nourse told Uncle was: "He's allowed to give only thirteen lashes, no more, without my permission."

I didn't want to go into the house, though we were welcomed. They knew all about us. Uncle was exclaimed over by Mr. Nourse for his accomplishments with birds. Dinner was waiting. There were only ten minutes to wash up and refresh ourselves.

Ralph was sent to the kitchen to eat, Earline to the slave quarters. Later she told us she had hoecakes made of cornmeal, taters roasted in the ashes, and ashcake cooked in the coals. No meat or greens, she said. Bacon was given out only on Saturdays. Or maybe the slaves would catch a possum or a rabbit. Or catch a fish in Sullivan's Creek.

Right off, Mr. Nourse showed that he didn't think much of women. After supper he told me to go into the parlor with his wife while he and Uncle took a tour of the place.

I didn't want to leave Uncle and he knew it.

"I'd like her to come with us," he told Mr. Nourse. "We've been traveling quite a bit. She's seen some things that have disquieted her. I'd like to keep her close to me."

"Spoilin' her good, are you?" Mr. Nourse said jokingly. But I could tell he meant it.

"If I have to betimes, yes," Uncle returned calmly.

"Thought we'd talk some men's talk."

"Like to, when she goes to bed," Uncle said.

So I went along with them. I saw the stables, the outbuildings, the meat house, the laundry, the blacksmith shop, the carpentry shop, the infirmary. Every known convenience to man was here. The plantation was a world of its own.

And then we saw the "nursery."

It was a cabin no different from the rest, with the usual dirt floor on which sat at least eight babies with two girls of about ten, tending them.

"They're watched carefully all day while the mamas work in the fields," Mr. Nourse said proudly, "and the girls take them out in the sunshine, too."

"Are they never held?" Uncle asked.

Mr. Nourse scowled. "Maybe your babies up North are held, Doctor, but we have no time for such piddle-waddle down here. The babies do just fine on their own."

Uncle told me later that babies who are never held don't grow up properlike, that it takes holding and hugging to make them whole inside, that he'd studied on it.

He did not argue the point with Mr. Nourse.

I was sent to bed early and it was then that I met Roselle, my nursemaid, who was another Tessa, yet even better. Was there a Tessa at every plantation, I wondered?

More than just help me get ready for bed, she had a brass tub full of water waiting for me in my room. I was to undress, she said.

"You-all must be god-awful messy from your journey. A nice bath would make you feel jus' fine."

Undress? In front of her?

"Now, I know what you're thinkin'. This here negro done bathed every female on this place an' even the master when he wuz sick. Now you just doan waste time bein' ashamed. The Lord done give us all the same body. You just come on now. I'll turn my back an' get the bed ready while you get outa your clothes an' get in the tub. Go on."

There was no way out of it. I had to do what she said. But the tub of warm, sudsy water did feel good.

"Anyways," she said as she came forward with a soft cloth to help bathe me, "there's things I gots to tell you, if'n you gonna be about this place."

"What things?" I asked.

"Well, first of all, I gots the power. Had it since I was a pickaninny. My mammy used to talk about signs alla time. There are some things the Lord wants all folks to know an' some He jus' wants a few to know. Fer instance, I knows 'bout Earline and her Ralph. I knows they wedded. An' I'se the onliest one 'round here now, 'sides that uncle-man of yours an' you who knows it."

I dropped my soap in the tub and had to hunt for it. It was a fine-smelling soap. Lavender. I made a great to-do over finding it, hiding my face from her. "Who told you?" I asked.

"Like I says, I gots the power, an' I wanna tell you, if'n you all wants that Ralph feller to get away from here alive, keep him, an' her, away from the voodoo meeting the slaves gonna have tomorrow night."

"The voodoo meeting?"

"Yes. They have one once a month. Tomorrow's the night. Doan you let that Earline person go. I see bad signs fer her there. An' that Ralph person, too. Course, they won't let him join in, him bein' white an' all, but he'll likely be there, watchin', and if'n Bench goes, just to keep an eye on things, there will be trouble. I got the word."

I nodded my head. "All right."

Roselle was starting to wash my hair. I thought for a moment that my head would come off she scrubbed so hard. "You-all got the prettiest hair," she commented. Then came the water poured over my head and I thought I would drown.

"I gots more to tell you," she went on. "Two more things. Fust, that bird yer uncle be lookin' for. I done seen it. 'T'other side of the woods. Near the stream. An' I knows it'll be back tomorrow night, just about dark."

"Ooh," I breathed. "Can I tell him?"

"You kin tell him anythin' I tell you. Course, bein' a man of science, he likely will say it's no-count, my power. Second thing. Now listen. There be two mens in the woods. Look like wild mens. They gots long hair down their backs and hair all over their faces. Scare the bejesus outa you. The back o' their shirts all bloody from livin' in the briar patches. They be runaways."

I waited for more. None came. "Why are you telling me this?" I asked.

"Jus' tellin' is all."

So she knew, too, about Uncle. Oh god, I must be careful with her, good to her. She knew everything!

While I contemplated the impossibility of all this, she rubbed my head dry. It felt good and I became sleepy, but then she told me one more thing.

"Doan you go takin' any chances 'round here," she warned. "Doan you go stickin' your pretty little nose in where it doan belong or you might get hurt. You hear me?"

I said yes.

"Now stand up and dry yourself."

I stood up, afraid not to. She wrapped a soft towel around me and I stepped out of the tub and dried myself while she lighted a fire in the hearth. Before I knew it I was in my nightdress, sitting before a fire, and she was drying my hair and rolling it in rags like Aunt Susan Elizabeth used to do. Then she made me kneel and say my prayers. For myself, for Earline and Ralph, for Uncle.

I had a feeling bad things were going to happen on this place. Worse than on any of the others.

Apparently Roselle thought so, too, because the next morning when she came to bring me a cup of coffee topped with cream and chocolate to sip while she unrolled my hair, she showed me what she had made for me.

It was a small red-flannel bag to wear around my neck with a red piece of knitting yarn. In it was a mixture of graveyard dust, ground-up frog, snakeskin, and mouse turd. "It will keep you safe from any danger," she told me. "I done blessed it. Tuck it inside your dress."

My dress buttoned with at least six buttons in front. There was a wide white collar, which helped to hide it, too.

"You look nice," Uncle said when I appeared belowstairs. "Who did your hair?"

"Roselle."

He noticed the lump under my white collar right off. "And what else did she give you? What's that you're wearing under your collar?" He found and fingered the red knitting yarn.

"It's for good luck, Uncle. Roselle said I'm going to need it today. It's a small red-flannel bag with good luck symbols in it."

I proceeded to recite what was in it.

"Take it off," he ordered.

We were at the foot of the stairway, alone in the hall outside the dining room.

"Please, Uncle, let me keep it on. Roselle said it's important that I wear it today. Please."

"You don't need rattlesnake skin to keep you safe. God, child, what's happening to you? Take it off."

I stamped my foot. "No." What could he do to me here? He hated scenes.

Abruptly he took me by the elbow and turned me around and commenced to push my hair aside and untie the knot of the red knitting yarn and pull on the bag. But it was entrenched inside my dress and wouldn't budge. Again he turned me around. "Unbutton the dress," he said.

He was angry now because he was thwarted, and he hated being thwarted.

"Here?" I asked.

He dragged me across the hall and into the library and closed the door.

There were tears in his eyes. "Unbutton the dress and take off the bag."

For the first time ever, I defied him. "No. Uncle, please, if something happens to me today it'll be your fault."

He would have no more. He started to unbutton the dress himself, all six tiny buttons. And there, just below my neck bone, was the errant bag. He pulled it off and stuffed it into his jacket pocket. "Button yourself," he ordered, and stood there while I did.

"You don't ride out with me today. I don't want you if you can't obey."

Oh, he was angry. He was like a little boy who'd lost at marbles. What was it Tessa had told me about men? *You be good to him. Men always need us women to be good to them. They act real brave, but they sometimes be more scared than us.*

Was Uncle making a show of bravery now, being angry with me? Was he more scared than I?

"It's Thursday," I made an attempt at humor. "You can beat me if you want."

He cast me a scowling glance. "Don't you bad-mouth me." The tone was warning.

"I didn't mean to bad-mouth, sir. I was just trying to find a way to say I'm sorry."

"Sorry won't do you any good right now. I don't want to see you for the rest of the day. Find something to do with yourself." He started for the door.

"Uncle, I've something important to tell you."

He turned with his hand on the knob. "Make it quick."

"There are two men in the woods." And I told him, in as few words as I could, about the two "mens" with hair down their backs and all over their faces.

He listened, no change of expression on his face. Then he just nodded slightly.

"The bird," I said, "has been seen on the other side of the woods. Near the stream."

"By whom?"

"Roselle," I told him dismally.

He turned, impatiently.

"Uncle, she knows things."

"What do you mean she *knows* things?"

"Sir, you don't have to believe me. She said the Ever-After Bird would be back tonight, just about dark. And she knew that Earline and Ralph are married."

"You told her this?"

"No, sir. She told me."

"How much else does she *know*?"

"That's all she told me, sir. And I told her nothing. I swear it."

"You don't have to swear. I believe you. Now come along. We're already late for breakfast. And remember what I said. I don't want to see you for the rest of the day."

Chapter Nineteen

NOW I WAS the one with tears in my eyes. I was silent during breakfast, though Uncle tried, once or twice, to pull me into the general conversation. I answered with the required yes, sir or no, sir to make him happy, but he was not happy, and when the meal was over he did not say good day to me. He said nothing.

I sat on the back veranda and watched him saddle up and make ready to leave. I knew all the moves, watched him tie on his equipment, his large notebook, his case with the drawing pencils, his ax, his sacks, his pine-knot torch in case he came back after dark, and what I knew he had hidden for when he met the men in the woods. A compass, maps, maybe even a razor and scissors so they could shave and cut their hair. Clothes they would steal from the drying lines of other plantations. He couldn't carry it all and not be under suspicion.

It would not be easy going alone.

Earline would stay. She had come up with some reason about being needed here, as there were three slaves down with the fever today and guests were expected at the big house for supper.

But I knew differently. I knew there was to be the voodoo dance tonight at which Earline and Ralph would receive their marriage blessing and she must make ready for it.

I should have told Uncle, but I didn't. I was angry with him for pushing me aside this day. Let him find out himself, now.

I just sat there on the veranda, hoping that at the last minute he'd relent and ask me to come along and help in Earline's place. But he did not. His resolution was all fired up. He had done it before on his own and he could do it again.

I watched him ride off. Something ached dreadfully inside me. Find yourself something to do today, he'd said. All right, I would.

The first thing I did was change into my riding habit and go into the kitchen and ask for some leftover muffins from breakfast to put into my haversack, for I was going for a ride. The cook generously gave me two muffins stuffed with ham and wrapped them in cabbage leaves, and I stuffed them in my haversack.

Into the haversack also went an apple and an orange and a few sticks of peppermint candy. I thanked her and went outside to the barn to ask for a horse.

His name was Slapbang and he was a fine-looking creature, almost as fine-looking as my Pelican. We headed right out, not in Uncle's direction but to the road that went by the fields where the cotton grew. There were some slaves picking cotton. In another field some were picking red potatoes.

I saw Bench, the overseer, in the cotton field, carrying his curled-up whip. Only thirteen lashes he was allowed to give, I reminded myself for some reason. No more without Mr. Nourse's permission.

I went on. Or rather Slapbang did. He seemed to know the way, past the cotton fields, past the cornfields, and into the pine barrens. The road grew more narrow. There was no one about. Should I be frightened? I could find my way back and if I couldn't, certainly Slapbang could.

And then I came upon two huts. There was no other word to describe them. Someone, no, two someones were living in them.

They were seated on rustic benches out front.

I could not immediately determine what they were. At first I thought they were Roselle's "wild men" in the woods, and then I decided no, for they were women dressed in long rags. They did not have beards, but they had long gray hair. They held canes, they smoked pipes, and when they stood up they were so bent over they looked like the gnomes in the fairy-tale books Aunt Susan Elizabeth had read to me when I was a child.

"Hello," I said, and I slipped off Slapbang so as not to frighten them. I held him by the reins and he quieted nicely.

They were very aged. They eyed me suspiciously at first, then they spoke, one at a time. Did I come from the plantation, they wanted to know.

"Yes, I'm a guest."

"My name be Salina," said one. "What be yourn?"

"CeCe."

"Mine be Cinda," the other one cackled. "I be ninety-nine years now. How old you be, child?"

"Fourteen in December."

"I had me fourteen chilluns," Cinda said. "Too old to work now, so we's live out here. You gots any victuals?"

"Please," Salina begged. "They send you wif any food?"

Immediately I reached into my haversack and drew out my food. How fortunate that there were two muffin sandwiches and two of everything. They considered it a feast.

They could scarce eat for lack of teeth, but they managed somehow, and in between munching they told me about the "old days" when Mr. Nourse's father ran the place, and when nobody was whipped, and when they were young and worked for old Mrs. Nourse in the big house.

"Now you sees our offsprings' offspring in the fields," Cinda told me.

And then, when I was getting ready to leave, they begged me to speak to Mr. Nourse for them. They needed new, warmer clothes for the winter. They needed regular visits with food.

"They send a slave wif food, but he or she eats it on the way," Cinda said.

"We cain't tell nobody," from Salina, "'cause nobody come out here to see us. Please, little CeCe, tell young Mr. Nourse, please."

Their cries echoed in my ears as I started back home.

I minded that, by the sun in the sky, I had stayed a long time at this place. The ride home was well over an hour. I would likely miss my noon meal. Would anybody miss me? Uncle wouldn't even know I was gone because he was gone, too. I never felt so alone or abandoned in the world as I rode back to the plantation.

And then, when I passed the cotton field where the negroes were picking, the very field where I'd seen Bench that morning, it happened.

Three negro women broke away from their picking and ran out into the road and accosted me. I had all I could do to hold Slapbang's reins so he wouldn't trample them to death.

"Oh, missee, you beg massa for us. Tell him we needs more time outa the fields after we deliver a baby."

"Oh, missee, tell massa we needs some coffee. Tell him we works so much better if'n we have coffee. An' some bacon. Oh, we ain't had bacon in so long."

"Oh, missee," from still a third, "please tell massa not to sell my husband off. I cain't live wifout my husband."

At that very moment Bench came charging over. "Git back in the field, alla you. And you!" He glared at me. "You git away from heah an' stop distractin' my help!"

"I've a right to ride by."

"You shudda kept on goin'!" He had grabbed by the arm the slave who had begged me to tell master not to sell off her husband. Now he dragged her back into the field. "I'm gonna teach you right heah and now not to stop your work. I'm gonna teach alla you not to botha people 'bout your troubles."

He threw her, facedown, on the ground. He uncurled his whip.

"No, Mr. Bench, please, please," she begged. And as she begged, the others begged with her, "Please, please, Mr. Bench, we didn't mean no harm."

He cracked his whip at them and they ran. Then he proceeded to whip the young woman who had begged for her husband.

I stood, holding Slapbang's reins, stunned. And I didn't know what was worse, the sound of the whip or the piteous cries of the young woman.

No more than thirteen, I told myself. *No more. Maybe less.*

I found myself counting.

The young woman stopped screaming at eight. She must have passed out.

Why didn't I do something?

Because I had no right.

Thirteen, fourteen, fifteen. Fourteen? Fifteen?

No more than thirteen. It was then that I did something.

First I tethered Slapbang to a nearby cottonwood tree. Then I ran to where Mr. Bench was still swinging back his whip. "You're not allowed to give more than thirteen!" I screamed at him. "I heard Mr. Nourse say so."

Mercifully, he stopped. "You dare question me? You little turd?"

"I know what Mr. Nourse said. And I'm going to tell him what you did."

"He'll take you for what you are. A liar."

"I'm not a liar. My uncle knows I'm not a liar."

"You keep your mouth shut, you little witch, or you'll hear from me. Now git outa heah." He gathered his whip in, though, and threw a bucket of water on the girl. She gasped and writhed in pain. I would have gone to her but he chased me away, threatening me with the very same whip.

I got onto Slapbang and took off down the road.

Is this what life was like on the underbelly of every plantation? Apparently it was. Apparently this is what all those people who had come to Papa in the middle of the night were running from.

How had he known?

And what about all the people who waded across the river to come to Uncle Alex?

And then I thought of Earline, and how many times she'd been whipped. So why then did she have to come on this expedition to know what it was like to be a slave and write about it? She'd been a slave once, as a child, hadn't she?

And then it came to me. As a child. In the big house. Perhaps she needed now to know what it was like to be a slave in the big house and quarters as a grown-up? How dared she come back, I wondered, after having got with child on a plantation?

All this, all I had seen, gave me a new appreciation of her I had treated her badly. I must make it up to her somehow. But how, without groveling? It wasn't in me to grovel.

I needed to talk to somebody. I needed Uncle desperately, but I dared not try to find him. And even if he made it home for supper, I dared not seek him out. His anger toward me was real.

I rode home slowly, knowing what I must do.

I needed to speak with Earline. I needed to warn her about the voodoo dance tonight, and what Roselle had told me. I owed her that.

But first I needed to eat. I was, as they said around here, about starved, having given over my noon meal to the old hags in their huts. Straightaway I made for the barns and instructed the boy waiting for Slapbang to feed and water him, and to keep him saddled, for I intended to use him again that afternoon.

Since I had missed the formal luncheon, I went into the kitchen and again the cook greeted me. "Ah, the little hungry one, once more. You like the lunch I send with you, chile?"

"Yes, auntie. But I didn't eat it. I came upon two very old ladies in their huts, far off beyond the cornfields, and they were starving. I gave it to them."

"Ah, the crooked old womens in their crooked old huts." She laughed. "They gets food outa everybody. How they doin'? Right pitiful, ain't they?"

"Yes. They need things. They're hungry."

"Massa send them vittles. Doan you worry 'bout them. They outa they heads half the time. You jus' sit your little self down an' I gonna fix you some vittles like you never done had before."

I sat. She gave me hot coffee, with the usual cream and shaved chocolate on top. She set down before me fish and eggs and bacon and waffles, and I couldn't eat half of it, but I tried. Then she sat on the other side of the wooden-plank table and looked at me.

"You'se a spunky little thing. I wuz bringin' some food from the kitchen into the server's hands this mornin' when I heard you talkin' back to your uncle in the hall there. In my day a little girl like you got spanked fer talkin' back to her elders like that."

I blushed. "Uncle doesn't hit me," I said.

"Then I kin ask you to do me a favor this afternoon and you won't git in no trouble?"

"What is it?"

"Since you like to give away food an' all. There's a cave, just short o' the woods, where you were this mornin'. You might o' passed it an' not seen it. Nobody knows it's there 'ceptin' a few of us. In it live the wife an' chilluns of Cicero, a field slave. She run off six years ago. She used to work in the big house. One day the missus give her a lotta loud talk and slap her. And she slap the missus back. Well, there was a ruckus. Missus said the master wuz gonna beat her. Well, Caline, that be her name, ran to her husband in the field. Cicero tell her to run off. Showed her the cave and tol' her to hide there an' she did. He bring her food. She stay, nigh onta years. He fix it up fer her, with a plank floor an' log walls an' he put a stove in there an' run a pipe out through the ground inta' the swamp. They cook only at night. He make her tables and beds and brung her quilts. Jus' like a house. They gots two chilluns there.

"Everybody brings 'em food. Jus' drop it off outside. Never go inside. Never see Caline. Jus' drop off the food. Now, if'n I fix a sack o' food, will you drop it off? Doan go to the cave. They be a bunch of cottonwood trees a bit before it. You drop it off there. Will you?"

I said yes, I would. She gave me directions to the cave. It turned out I had passed it that very morning and I knew my way. I remembered the cottonwood trees, too.

I was to tell no one. I took the sack, went back to the barn for Slapbang, mounted him, and rode off again on my second adventure of the day.

Chapter Twenty

EARLINE HELPED serve supper. I watched her come in and out of the dining room with steaming platters of meat and fish and other delicacies and wondered what would happen if I excused myself and ran after her and told her not to go to that voodoo meeting tonight.

I would make a disgrace of myself in front of all those guests, jumping up like that to run and talk to one of the negro maids. Oh, that would have gone over fine when they told Uncle Alex, wouldn't it? As if I weren't in enough trouble.

I told myself to be satisfied with what I'd done that day. After all, I'd delivered the sack of food to the cottonwood trees for Caline and her family, hadn't I? And not been discovered. I felt good about myself for having done that. Why I'd just ridden over the open land, past the cornfields and cotton fields, under the hard blue sky, and when I came to the cottonwood trees, I paused for a minute to listen to the birds and the cicadas droning in the sun and then, carelessly dropped the sack of food and rode on.

I never looked back.

The ride home had been lonely and hot. I missed Uncle Alex and wondered if he'd catch the Ever-After Bird this day. And if he did, would I miss seeing it?

And now, here I was, finishing up our dinner, making senseless talk with the Nourses, enjoying coffee and cake with whipped cream and fresh peaches in rum at a table set with the whitest of cloths and the brightest of silverware and crystal and china from England and I wondered if Caline and her children were enjoying their meat and bread and fruit in their primitive cave.

Someone said something to me about Uncle Alex and his "bird chasing." I gave an answer and smiled.

It was after supper that I discreetly followed Earline into the detached kitchen.

"I need to talk to you," I told her.

"You don't belong in here," she said in a whispered snarl. "You trying to ruin everything?"

I knew there was no time to waste on niceties. "Don't you and Ralph go to the voodoo dance tonight. Or bad things will happen."

"Oh?" Her almond-shaped eyes opened wide. "And you got this information where?"

"From Roselle."

"Oh, I forgot, she has the gift."

"Earline, please. I know we've argued in the past. But yes, Roselle does have the gift. She knows things. I don't know how. But I believe her. And I consider it my duty to warn you."

"Consider me warned then. And get out of this kitchen before somebody spills gravy on that nice pink silk of yours. Go on, go."

I hesitated. She wasn't going to take me seriously. Which meant I was going to have to follow her at a discreet distance and make sure everything was all right.

I CHANGED OUT of my pink silk and white slipper-shoes into a calico dress and my sturdy lace-up boots. You had to be dressed for it if you were going to go to a voodoo dance.

THROUGH THE RUSHES and swaying grasses I followed the tall, dark, sinewy forms ahead of me. I didn't know where I was going, but I figured they did.

It was murky and I picked up my skirts and had all I could do to keep from falling. The light from their pine-knot torches was sufficient, somehow, to illuminate my path. In the distance I heard drums. All around me I sensed excitement.

Where were Earline and Ralph? I didn't know. I really didn't know anyone around me. And then I heard a breathless Roselle coming up behind me. "You there, little white girl, where you think you goin'?"

"To see the dance."

"It be late. That uncle of yourn ain't come back yet, but when he do he be lookin' fer you. What he gonna do when you ain't about?"

I hadn't given it a thought. Well, he hadn't wanted to see me all day, he'd said. So let him worry a little bit now.

Of course, that was bravado talking, not me. I really didn't feel that way. Inside I was fearful of what Uncle would say if I wasn't in the plantation house when he returned. But I'd thrown my lot in with these people now. It was too late to turn around and go back. I had no pine-knot torch. I'd fall in a hole and break a leg. I had to keep on going. And if I had to suffer another bawling out, well then, so be it.

And then up ahead I saw the fire, its sparks melting into the darkness, a crowd of people all around it, and all around Ralph and Earline.

Some wore headdresses. Some of the women had taken off the tops of their dresses and at first I was embarrassed, but after a while I scarce noticed. Earline, of course, was not about to do this. She just stood there holding Ralph's hand, while the others formed a circle around her and danced, and two men played the drums and everyone chanted.

I stayed in the background in the tall grasses. The whole thing was like a bad dream, like the ones I would get after having too much chocolate cake before going to bed. And then soon the dancing and the chanting stopped and another man came into the circle with a broom and set it down before Earline and Ralph, and before I knew what was happening the two of them jumped over it and everyone clapped. The man, who I assumed was some kind of a medicine man or reverend, began chanting over them. Then he sprinkled them with powder out of a bottle, after which he dashed them with water from another bottle.

He was dressed in the plain clothes of a present-day reverend. And no sooner had he done his sprinkling than there was a terrible shout from behind me and Bench burst past me and into the crowd.

"How many times I gotta tell y'all I don't stand fer no voodoo 'round heah?" He cracked his whip indiscriminately and everyone screamed and dispersed.

"Put that fire out!" he ordered. "You ain't gonna leave it burn all night an' set the whole place ablaze. You! Henry! George! Sulpha! Cicero! Get those buckets! Get down to the stream over theah and put that fire out! Now!" More cracking of the whip.

Instead of running, Ralph and Earline just stood there talking with the reverend. And Bench grabbed them both, curling his whip around them.

"I heared you two wuz married. So it be true. White and darkie. Well we doan counter with such down heah. An' you both gonna pay fer it. Tonight. I got the massa's permission. Heah! Randee!"

"Yessuh."

"You want youself a whippin' this night that'll make you unconscious fer a week?"

"Nosuh."

"Then you help me out. You heah?"

"Yessuh, I helps."

"You take this white fella, Ralph, an' you tie him up on that ol' oak tree out behind the barn. You knows the one."

"Yessuh. The hangin' tree."

"No, no," Earline begged. "Please don't hang him. Please!"

"Who said anythin' 'bout hangin', missy? I gots more fun in mind. Anyways, I gots to attend to you, first. Come along now lak a good girl. You gonna find out what it means to wed a white man. Uppity darkie like you gonna find out, yessuh."

"Leave her be!" I stepped forward then. "Or I'll tell my uncle."

"Ah." He stopped, Earline in tow. "The little scallywag. Wait'll your uncle finds out you be down here tonight. You'll get your own whippin', doan worry."

"CeCe, go find Dr. Alex," Earline begged. "Please."

I ran. The last I saw her, Bench was dragging her away.

Chapter Twenty-One

IT SEEMS AS IF I ran all the way back to the plantation barnyard to see if Uncle Alex was back yet. First I checked the barn to ask whether his horse had been returned. It hadn't. My heart fell. How late would he stay out? How far was the place where Roselle had said the Ever-After Bird could be seen just about dark. That meant dusk.

It was well after dusk now. He should be back any minute. But wait, what was that commotion down by the blacksmith shop? People were gathering around.

And there was Bench. With Earline in tow.

He was tying her hands up around a pole and I could hear her begging.

He was going to whip her!

I ran down the dusty road, past the laundry, the corncrib, the nursery, the infirmary, the meat house, the carpentry shop. I pushed my way through the crowd at the blacksmith shop. Earline was crying now.

Bench had ripped down the top part of her dress to expose her back.

There were scars on her back from previous whippings. Raised scars from when she had been on that plantation in her teen years, the age I was now.

Bench stood there, running the whip through one hand, holding it with the other. The crowd of negroes stood silent and mournful, afraid to stay, afraid to leave. Likely he had ordered them to stay.

Earline was sobbing quietly, likely remembering all those other whippings.

"You can't!" I ran over to Bench. I was not afraid. What could he do to me? "You can't. She belongs to my uncle Alex, not to Mr. Nourse. You haven't the right. She isn't yours. You can't," I said again.

"Oh, can't I? Well, little girl, she's dishonored every code we have down heah. An' she's gonna pay fer it. Any plantation owner or overseer would say the same thing."

"You *can't,*" I said again. "She's been whipped before. Can't you see?"

"Well she musta deserved it then."

I reached for his whip. "I'm not going to let you do it."

"Watch yerself, little girl, or you'll find yerself up there in her place."

He gave me the idea. If I was up there, my arms wrapped around Earline, he couldn't do it, could he? I could stall him off until Uncle Alex got back, and surely he'd be back any minute. So I took the advantage. I ran the short distance between us and Earline. I wrapped my arms around her trembling body. I hugged her.

"I'm here, Earline," I said. "I'm here. He can't hurt you now."

She was sobbing, trembling. "CeCe, go away. He'll hurt you, too."

"He doesn't dare. He doesn't dare whip a white girl."

"The man is crazy, CeCe. He dares to do anything."

I nuzzled my face into her neck. "I owe this to you, Earline. I know I was wrong the way I treated you. I was wrong about a lot of things. And I'm going to make it up to you now."

At that moment there was a crunching of footsteps behind me and I felt an ugly presence. Bench.

"You wants it, little girl, you gots it," he said. And he took my hands and tied them around the post, around Earline's body. So tightly he tied them that my wrists hurt.

"What are you doing?" I demanded.

"Givin' you what you wants. What that uncle of

yours likely nevah give you. Now you gonna learn." And he stepped behind me and in one swift motion took the collar of my blue calico dress and ripped it down, exposing my back and my arms.

There came an "ooh" murmur from the crowd.

"Shut up," he told them.

And then he cracked his whip. Just short of me. I couldn't believe it. I couldn't believe what was about to happen.

Chapter Twenty-Two

THE FIRST searing taste of fire bit into my back and tore across it like flame from a pine-knot torch. I remember screaming, "Uncle Alex! Uncle Alex!"

But no Uncle Alex came.

I heard the whistle of the whip, heard it in my ears as the second crackling bit of leather cut into my back and sides. I felt the blood dripping and thought, *No pain could be as bad as this, not even childbirth.*

"I'm going to faint," I mumbled to Earline.

"Faint," she said, "do."

Blackness filled my eyes. Shooting sparks of light. But the merciful darkness of fainting never came.

He was drawing his whip in for a third strike. I knew the sound of it by now, and it struck me, and I screamed just when another sound permeated my ears. The sound of horse's hooves, the cries of the crowd, and the good, plain curses of my uncle Alex as he likely threw himself off the horse and attacked Bench.

There was scuffling, beating sounds, punching sounds, and never had I heard such wonderful curses as those Uncle Alex bestowed on Bench. I didn't know he knew such words. Oh, they were heavenly blessings. Of course I couldn't see. I could scarce turn my head around, and when I tried, my back and neck hurt so bad that tears came to my eyes.

But I did see that Bench was on the ground. And that he wasn't about to get up again for a while. Uncle Alex had him tied up with his own whip.

Next thing I knew, Uncle Alex was untying my hands and Earline's and saying things like, child, how did you get into this situation, and, Earline, are you all right, and fix your dress, because Earline hadn't been touched by the whip. I tried to fix mine but couldn't. Because I couldn't stand up straight. I slumped. All I could think of was holding that dress up in front of me so Uncle Alex and others wouldn't see my bosoms. Because my bosoms were quite respectable for a thirteen-year-old. And then the next thing I knew he was picking me up in his arms and somebody, likely Earline, pulled my dress up in front and I saw the wonderful blackness inside my eyelids, but I did not faint, because I was in Uncle Alex's arms and I wanted to make sure Bench wouldn't come and take me out of them.

I RECOLLECT THE day I told myself that if I were ever run over by a carriage and Uncle Alex had to rip off my clothes it would be all right.

Well, this was worse than being run over by a carriage, I hurt so. And I was humiliated, not by what Uncle did to me but by what Bench had done to me in front of all those people. I was coming out of the shock of it by the time we got to his room where his doctor's things were and he laid me on his bed, and the pain was growing more intense. I started to sob uncontrollably, and the first thing Uncle did was give me a powder and send downstairs for some rum.

The Nourses came upstairs, he and she. I was lying on my stomach on Uncle's bed, with my dress and chemise pulled down to my waist, and Roselle was handing Uncle clean wet cloths to bathe my back with. And though his hands were gentle, I still cried at his touch.

The Nourses brought the rum.

"I don't want anybody else in here," I said between sobs to Uncle.

He thanked them for the rum and said he would speak to them later.

"I assure you Bench will be fired," Mr. Nourse told him.

"Get him off the place today," Uncle told him, "or I may shoot him."

They left. Uncle cleaned the blood off my back. "I don't know whether dusting with morphine will be sufficient," Uncle told Roselle.

"I gots some remedy we use 'round here fer whippings," she said.

"What is it?" he asked.

"Buzzard's grease stewed up in lard. I gots it all ready in a jar."

"Does it work?" Uncle asked.

"Best for whippings," she answered. "Cure the back in no time. Then you kin dust some o' your morphine on toppa that fer the pain."

They agreed, and she went to get her buzzard's grease stewed up in lard and Uncle spread it on my wounds. It did take out the sting. And afterward he sprinkled on his morphine dust and I scarce felt a thing. Then he went out of the room to give me my privacy, and Roselle bathed the rest of me and combed my hair and helped me into the softest of my nightgowns.

The combination of the laudanum and the rum put me into a half sleep. I sensed people walking around me.

I heard the murmurings of talk, but I could not make out what people were saying.

I heard a scream. It was Earline's voice, I was sure of it. Was she being whipped after all? I tried to rouse myself, but did not consider it worth the effort. I was in a pleasant place for the first time in a long time. I felt Uncle's hand on my head, smoothing back my hair, felt his presence, knew he was sitting there next to me.

And then I heard Earline sobbing, "Oh, Dr. Alex, he's dead, he's dead."

I opened my eyes and turned my head.

Earline was kneeling on the floor at Uncle's feet, her head on his lap. He was smoothing down her hair. "I'm sorry, child, I'm sorry." And then he did some more of that fancy cussing of his.

"What kind of people are they breeding down here anyway?" It was the first time I noticed the cut above his left eye. The swelling on his right cheekbone. The swollen knuckles on his right hand. He hadn't come out of the fight with Bench unscathed.

"They said it was Randee," Earline was saying. "Bench told him to take Ralph to the hanging tree behind the barn and tie him up or he'd whip Randee into a week of unconsciousness. Randee wanted to please Bench. So he hanged Ralph. He's dead."

Uncle Alex leaned down to comfort Earline. She clung to him and he let her sob.

"Who's dead?" I asked in a scratchy voice.

They both looked at me. "Ralph," Earline hiccupped it out. "They hanged him. My Ralph is dead, CeCe." She left Uncle Alex and crawled over to my bedside and embraced me. "Oh, CeCe, they hanged him while they were whipping you. Oh, CeCe, my love is gone. Gone!"

Uncle had gotten up to fetch something from his doctor's bag. He brought it over with a small glass of rum and offered it to Earline.

"No," she said. "No. I must cry for Ralph. I must mourn."

Uncle set down the glass and the powder just as Roselle came into the room. He held Earline by the shoulders, and together he and Roselle forced the powder and rum down her throat. At first Earline gagged, but then she took it. Then Uncle picked her up and carried her into the room she shared with me, where Roselle likely put her to bed.

He did not come back for a good twenty minutes. When he did come, he checked his pocket watch. "It's late," he said. "Near ten. Time for you to go to bed."

In his hand he had a gilt cage.

In it was a bird. It was scarlet in color, and it had a long, narrow, curved beak. Its legs, too, were long and a bit curved, with three claws in front and one in back.

Though it hurt, I sat up. I knelt on the bed. "Uncle Alex, is it?"

"It's the Ever-After Bird, CeCe. Otherwise known as the scarlet ibis. A rare bird in these parts."

Tears came to my eyes.

"Has anybody seen it but me?"

"The Nourses. They gave me the cage. I brought him home in a sack. Came home to this ruckus and Mr. Nourse took him right into the house and put him in the cage. I don't know whether to celebrate him or curse him. If I hadn't been away this night, all this wouldn't have happened."

I fell silent. We looked at each other. "I was trying to keep Bench from whipping Earline, Uncle Alex. I thought if I threw myself around her, he wouldn't do it. I never thought he would whip me."

He nodded. "I don't know whether to scold you or hug you, CeCe. But you did a good thing for Earline. For that I thank you."

He said it so tenderly, tears came to my eyes. I lowered my head. "What are you going to do with the bird, Uncle Alex?"

He set the cage down on the floor and sat in one of the stuffed chairs by the bedside. "Can you come and sit in my lap?" he asked.

I eased myself off the bed and across the space between us. He lifted me onto his knee. "What do you want me to do with him?"

"Well, I understand. If you are going to paint him you have to kill him. You have to put a knife in his heart. I understand that, Uncle Alex."

"Would you rather I let him go free?"

I looked at him, into the blue eyes. They were deep with caring. "Would you do that?"

"I'd do it if you asked me to, CeCe. I'd do it for you. For what you've been through. I'd give him his freedom, yes."

I swallowed carefully. He meant it.

"There are other Ever-After Birds," he said. "I can come south again."

I bit my lower lip. I looked at the bird in the cage. "Could we show him to the slaves first?" I asked.

"We can do better than that," he said. "We can let him free in front of them. And Earline. How would you like that?"

"I'd like it fine," I said. "Can we do it tomorrow?"

"Tomorrow will be just fine," he said.

Chapter Twenty-Three

I DID NOT WANT to go downstairs and into the dining room for breakfast the next morning. Not even after Roselle had fixed my hair and put on my lightest dress that buttoned down back so Uncle could check my wounds.

"You must come sooner or later," he told me, applying more of Roselle's remedy and then the morphine dust. "It isn't you who should be ashamed. It's the Nourses, for having such a beast for an overseer."

"I can't help how I feel, Uncle."

"You should feel proud. You stepped in and saved Earline. I'm proud of you."

Slowly and carefully, he buttoned the dress in back.

"Uncle," I asked, "why do you look so terrible? Didn't you sleep last night?" The dress was buttoned. I turned to look at him. His eyes were red rimmed and bleary.

He looked sheepish. "I'm a madman," he confessed. "I stayed up all night and sketched that damned bird, CeCe. I can't just let him go without sketching him."

"In the cage?"

"Yes."

He looked so awkward, so little-boyish, that I had to hug him then. "All right, Uncle, I'll come down to breakfast. For you," I said.

"Good. And thank you for taking pity on me. Remember, I still have Earline to deal with. And Ralph to bury. And a new driver to hire before we can leave this godforsaken place," he said.

SOMEHOW, BY SOME underground method that worked on plantations, word had gotten out that Uncle was to free the Ever-After Bird. The slaves—house, field hands, barn and carpenter workers, blacksmith, laundresses, all of them—had gathered in the barnyard and were steadfastly waiting when we came out into the blue and gold morning.

Uncle bore the gilt cage in one hand. In the other he held Earline by the arm. Even she would not miss this. For it meant as much to her, seeing this bird, as it did to the still-bound servants.

They gathered round, in their tattered clothing, as Uncle held the cage for all to see the scarlet ibis.

"Don't come too close," he cautioned. "You don't want to frighten him. As a matter of fact, why don't you all line up and pass by one at a time and take a good look."

They did so, in an orderly fashion, exclaiming their *oohs* and *aahs*.

Inside his cage, the ibis preened and stretched. They wanted to feed him. Uncle said no.

One or two whispered to the bird. I heard the words *soon*, and *ever after*, and *we's be free*.

Tears came to my eyes.

One or two of them spoke to Uncle. Hesitantly. "That Bench be gone, suh?"

"Yes," Uncle answered, softly. "He was fired and sent off the property yesterday."

One or two of them spoke to me. They called me "sweet little thing" and "precious chile" and "God's own."

One of the women asked Uncle if she could touch me on the top of the head. He said yes, so she did, mumbling some words as she did so.

When they all had filed by, they took their places in a sort of circle around us, and Uncle cleared his throat. "We'll remember all of you," he promised. "Can we ask all of you to come to Ralph's funeral tonight and sing some spirituals for us?"

Yes, oh yes, they would come. Oh yes, they would sing.

Now, Uncle told them, he was going to let the Ever-After Bird go. And without further ado he picked up the cage, which he had set on the ground, and held it high. It glittered in the sunlight. Uncle opened the cage door. For a second or two the bird did not get out. He just sat there looking at everyone.

Uncle tapped the bottom of the cage gently and the bird came to the edge of it and stood there, looking around at everyone as if to say, "I fly away for all of you."

And then he raised his wings and flew. Up, up, into the sky, he flew. Not too far up, but just enough to go where he wanted to go. He knew where he was going, too. Toward the woods and the river. Over the fields.

Away from all this.

The slaves started to sing. The song was about flying away.

Uncle put his arm around my shoulder, lightly enough so it wouldn't hurt my wounds, and held me close.

We waited there until the Ever-After Bird was gone.

Chapter Twenty-Four

WE STAYED one more day at the Nourse plantation, long enough to bury Ralph.

The negroes sang their spirituals and, much to Uncle's and my surprise, Earline held up at the ceremony and did not collapse as we thought she would.

Had Uncle given her something? No matter, that was the way of it. Only silent tears came down her face.

I saw Uncle's rendering of the Ever-After Bird, and it was more than beautiful. It would, he told me, go into his *Birds of Georgia* book. He already had enough subscribers and the books would be published soon in New York. He carefully put the drawing away in the tin box with the others he'd sketched on the trip, and the next day we were ready to take our leave and go home. This time he'd hired a black driver.

No, *hired* was not the proper word. He'd purchased a quiet, dignified, elderly negro named Callum from Mr. Nourse. The man would soon be too old to work about the place anymore but was good with horses. Uncle would give him his freedom, and he would work for pay around our place in Ohio. Of course Uncle didn't tell the Nourses that.

We made the journey back home with no mishaps. I did not even get sick on the boat. When we got home the trees were starting to turn for it was September now. Aunt Elise was waiting in her chair with wheels on the front lawn, with Horace the turkey and the dogs next to her. Uncle picked her right up out of that chair and held her so close I thought he would crush her. He kissed her unashamedly, right there in front of us. Then, just like in the romance novels, he carried her up the stairs of the porch, into the house, and up to their room. They didn't come down for a long time.

My back still hurt for a while, so Aunt Elise took over putting the potion that Roselle had given us on it. And we still used the morphine. Uncle said I would have scars the rest of my life, like Earline, and I cried because I would never be able to wear a dress cut low in back. But Aunt Elise told me she'd make me a beautiful gown cut low in front, that men preferred it that way, anyway. And

Uncle said not too low. After all, he said, I was almost a woman now.

I was a woman. Because as soon as we got home I got my woman's time of the month. I know you aren't supposed to talk about it, but I told Aunt Elise and then, in a moment of need, I told Uncle Alex. Both because I wanted him to know and because I was in pain. He gave a small smile and offered me a powder and said thereafter I could find them in his surgery in a certain place, so I wouldn't have to come to him all the time and I could keep my privacy. And he trusted me not to abuse the privilege. That's what I mean about Uncle Alex. That's the kind of thing that makes me love him.

Earline went back to Oberlin and wrote her paper on her experiences, and in part of it she told how I took the whipping for her. I was so proud I thought I would burst. She got the very best of grades and she graduated, like Lucy Stanton before her, with a four-year degree in a literary course of study. She went on for her master's degree and then to teach. We are very proud of her.

Uncle Alex and Aunt Elise and I went back to our farm to visit shortly after we got home that fall. Aunt Susan Elizabeth was failing. So we stayed for a while and Uncle Alex wanted to bring her back to Ohio, but she wouldn't come. So he got a woman to come and stay with her.

The place looked so small. I couldn't understand why, until Uncle told me that's the way home always looks when you go back to it after you're grown up and you've been away and traveled and done things.

My room seemed to close in on me, making me dizzy. Had I once come here for refuge? I thought of all the places I'd been, all the things I'd seen, and the people I'd met. And I couldn't wait to get out of there.

Uncle made me visit my papa's grave. And just like before, leave flowers on it. I couldn't help thinking what I'd been like last time, and what I was like now.

Uncle had my dog and cat shipped back, by stage, to Ohio.

Aunt Susan Elizabeth died in early spring and we made another trip back home to visit and to bury her next to Papa. And that summer Uncle Alex took me and Aunt Elise on a trip to England to meet with his subscribers after his book came out. They gave him a party in London, in honor of the publication of his book, attended by so many naturalists and professors and businessmen who made such a fuss over him that Uncle said in a self-mocking way that he ought to get himself a coach-and-six and ride through the streets of Ripley, Ohio, when he got home.

All the beautiful women wanted to dance with Uncle

at the party, but he wouldn't dance because Aunt Elise couldn't. She had to push him, to make him dance. And he did dance beautifully.

He danced with me. "I see the gown is cut sufficiently low in front to make up for the back," he teased.

"But not too low, Uncle," I teased back. After all, I was fourteen and a half now. I'd been corresponding, regularly, with Robert.

"Low enough," he countered.

"Aunt Elise made it. And she approves."

"Women," he said, "always conspire. And incidentally, we never did have our talk about boys."

"Maybe we'll have time after I'm married," I told him.

"Which won't be for quite a while yet, I hope."

It wasn't. Robert came north to go to Princeton and came to visit and we, with Uncle's permission, became betrothed. Uncle and I never did have that talk about boys. It became a joke between us, a sort of pact, just like the low-cut dress in front and the powders in his surgery.

I went to Oberlin, as he wanted. When I graduated in 1859, Robert wanted me to marry him but I couldn't bring myself to go south again and relive all that agony and he had to run the plantation for his older sister. We remained betrothed, until we could figure out what to do. We again corresponded.

The War between the States came. Robert went for a soldier. Uncle became a captain with the Union army at thirty-eight. He cut off arms and legs. He attended the dying, sometimes on both sides. I stayed home with Aunt Elise.

Robert was killed at Gettysburg in 1863. I was just twenty-five and planning on settling down and becoming an old maid. Uncle, a major now, was home on leave, worn out mentally and physically from Gettysburg, when a group of Union army soldiers stopped by our house on the Ohio River as they tended to do, wounded and hurting. Aunt Elise and Nancy were accustomed to tending them. Only now Uncle did.

There was one by the name of William. He'd been shot in the leg at Gettysburg, and he was on his way home to Indiana, limping pitifully. Uncle wanted to take the leg off.

"Please, miss," he begged, "don't let the major take my leg off. Please, he seems to dote on you. Ask him to give me a chance."

I asked. Uncle complied. The leg stayed. So did William. To heal at first, and then to visit. And then, later, to work off the debt he said he owed Uncle, which

Uncle let him do because he knew the real reason he was staying was because of me.

They'd come in July. We, William and I, wed at Christmastime. In Uncle's house. Uncle and I never did have that talk about boys.

Uncle Renaldo because he knew the real reason he was staying was because of me.

The end came in July. We, William and I, were at [illegible] in [illegible]'s house. Uncle and I never did have that talk about love.

Author's Note

A BOOK NEVER comes to me in one whole piece, but in little bits and pieces that must, in the end, fit together like the parts of a picture puzzle. Usually some of the more obscure bits don't present themselves until I am well into the telling of the tale.

First comes the subject itself. That is usually something that has been "gnawing at my brain" for quite a while, and it is up to me to figure out how I want to present it.

It can be a tantalizing matter. In this case, I wanted to write a book based on a famous painting that everyone in this country would recognize, but all I could think of was birds. How many of us are familiar with paintings of birds, though we may not be experts on the species? Birds, somehow, give us happiness and hope.

It was then that the plot started to fall together for me. I remembered reading a line or so in one of my many factual books on slavery about a young Canadian physician named Dr. Alexander Ross who was, pre–Civil War times, one of the world's leading ornithologists (a person who studies birds). Dr. Alex, as I call him, visited the United States regularly to stay at some of the most successful plantations in the South, where he was a distinguished guest.

While he was a guest at these prominent plantations, he wandered about, supposedly to study and sketch his birds. Actually, he was moving among the slaves, giving them information about the Underground Railroad, about routes north, about safe houses along the way. He also gave them small amounts of money.

He was never discovered.

Dr. Alexander Ross was, in part, the role model for Uncle Alex in my book. But, though I searched and searched, I could find no more about him. Fine. The rest was up to me to fill in then. He was only part of my character. I would delve further into the most famous of ornithologists, John James Audubon. I studied Audubon's life to learn about the craft, about what tools ornithologists used, how they went after their prey, and I became fascinated by the accomplishments of this eminent man.

The third role model I incorporated into Uncle Alex was John Abbot, whose *Birds of Georgia* educated me as to exactly what birds Uncle Alex must come across in Georgia, a description thereof, and their Latin names.

As with most of my books, the characters took on life as the writing progressed. Earline took on an attitude all her own. Ralph, the driver, who entered the story as a minor character, quickly assumed importance and took on a major role as the writing grew stronger.

This is not unusual for my books. My characters go their own way and I cannot control them. This means I must follow and I do my best.

Extensive reading about Georgia in this pre–Civil War time period was necessary, of course. It was still a relatively primitive Georgia, and all the books in my bibliography will give credence to that fact.

Most of the cruel scenes of slavery are taken from record. In truth they are even somewhat whitewashed. The next time you look at a bird, remember, it is so much more than a bird. It has a history, just like humans do. It even has hopes and aspirations.

Bibliography

Anadolu-Okur, Nilgun. *Underground Railroad and Abolitionists of Pennsylvania.* Philadelphia: Temple University, 2002.

Audubon, John James. *The Audubon Reader.* Edited by Richard Rhodes. New York: Alfred A. Knopf, 2006.

Burke, Emily. *Pleasure and Pain.* Savannah: The Beehive Press, 1991.

Chadwick, Bruce. *Traveling the Underground Railroad.* Secaucus, N.J.: Carol Publishing Group, 1999.

Kemble, Frances Anne. *Journal of a Residence on a Georgian Plantation.* Savannah: The Beehive Press, 1992.

Killion, Ronald, and Charles Waller, eds. *Slavery Time When I Was Chillun Down on Marster's Plantation: Interviews with Georgia Slaves.* Savannah: The Beehive Press, 2002.

Lane, Mills. *Neither More Nor Less Than Men: Slavery in Georgia.* Savannah: The Beehive Press, 1993.

———. *The Rambler in Georgia: Desultory Observations on the Situation, Extent, Climate, Population, Manners, Customs, Commerce, Constitution, Government of the State from the Revolution to the Civil War Recorded by Thirteen Travellers.* Savannah: The Beehive Press, 1990.

Rhodes, Richard. *John James Audubon: The Making of an American.* New York: Random House, 2006.

Rogers-Price, Vivian. *John Abbot's Birds of Georgia.* Savannah: The Beehive Press, 1997.

Tobin, Jacqueline L., and Raymond G. Dobard, Ph.D. *Hidden in Plain View: A Secret Story of Quilts and the Underground Railroad.* New York: Random House, 1999.